Richard A. Frank

LIGHT

LIGHT

Copyright © 2020 by **Richard A. Frank**
All rights reserved.
richardafrank63@gmail.com

This is a work of fiction. Names, characters, businesses, places, events, locales, and incidents are either the product of the author's imagination or used in a fictitious manner. Any resemblance to actual persons, living or dead, or actual events, is purely coincidental. The author is not responsible for any interpretation of the content of this work of fiction.

All rights reserved.

First Printing: June, 2021

ISBN: 978-1-6780-8632-9

Publisher: **Roman Six Publishing**
                        Tanki Flip 52 A
                        Noord,
                        Aruba
                        romansixpublishing@gmail.com

Layout & Cover Design: **Vivienno L. Frank Jr.**

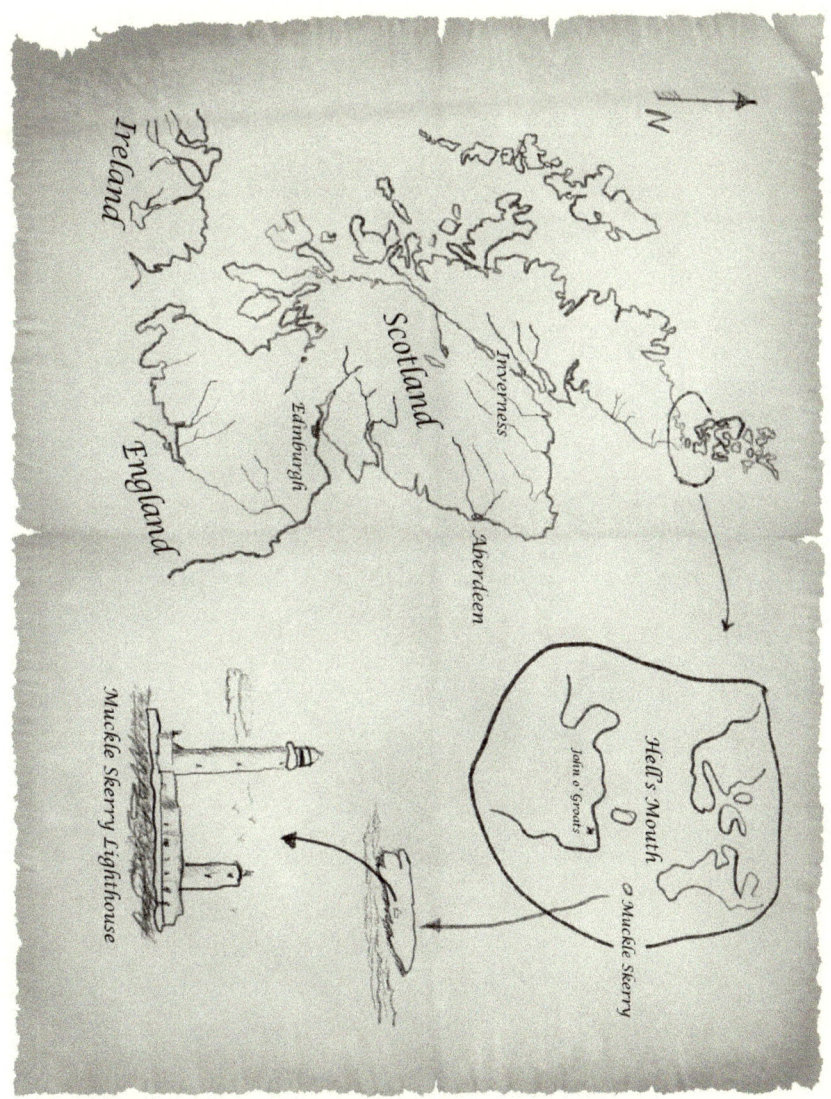

Courtesy of the Muckle Skerry Archives at The John o' Groats Foundation.

LIGHT

Light

'The Thebes House', by Alfred Reid. Courtesy of the 'Orphanage Collection' at the Aberdeen Heritage Centre, Aberdeen, Scotland.

I

Aberdeen, Scotland, autumn 1950 — There is a light knock on the door. Mother Agnes turns around and invites the knocker to come in: "Come in, the door is open". The heavy wooden door squeaks open, and a skinny young man enters the room and slowly makes his way to the desk. The room is spacious, but there hangs a clammy odor of old books. Mother Agnes, stern faced, motions the young man to take a seat.

"How long have you been with us, Jimmy?" asks the Mother Superior of the Poor Sisters of Thebes.

"Ten years, Mother," answers Jimmy in a low voice.

"Ten years, yes, time goes by so fast, doesn't it my son?" Mother Agnes sits down behind her desk. Jimmy remains quiet. The Mother Superior opens a thick book and starts to leaf through the pages.

"Ah, here you are, James Evans, arrived and registered in the orphanage on December 24, 1940, age six." She takes a pen, inks the point, and scribbles something in the book.

"So, there it is. You are being discharged from the orphanage my son. We found a well suited job for you," says Mother Agnes while slamming the book shut. Jimmy looks at the Mother Superior with bewildered eyes.

"Discharged, Mother?" he asks in disbelieve but with a tinge of relief in his voice.

"Yes, Jimmy. God helped Father Murray to find you a well-fitting job. You're sixteen years of age laddie: a young man ready to make himself useful to the world. You'll find this an opportunity of a lifetime. Now, start packing your things. Father Murray will be picking you up tomorrow morning at six o' clock to escort you by train to Inverness. Dismiss!" Mother Agnes laconically waves her hand shooing Jim away.

Jim leaves Mother's office and stands for a moment in the hallway. His heart beats fast and his mind is in utter turmoil. On the one hand Jim is jubilant that he is finally leaving this miserable place called the Thebes House on Cadbury Street, but on the other hand he is fearful to leave because he has never been to any other place than the surroundings of Aberdeen. Except for the usual house chores in the orphanage, Jim has never worked on his own on anything. The dark hallways of Thebes House are somber and oppressing. The crucifixes on the walls, the statues of saints, the chapel, the rigid daily routine of prayer and confession, all of that means nothing to Jim. The moldy smell in the hallways is disgusting. Slowly Jim walks to the stairs as if caught up in a dream. Memories of some happy times with his fellow orphans flash by in his mind but are immediately followed by some dreary and awful memories of horrid things he has witnessed and suffered in these dwellings. Jim shakes his head as if to toss those dreadful memories out of his mind and runs up the stairs. At the top of the stairs he meets Herbert, a fellow orphan and good friend.

"What's the hurry?" asks Herbert in a hushed voice. Loud talking or laughing is punishable in the Thebes House. Jim smiles and pulls Herbert close to him.

"I'm leaving this bloody place!" replies Jim excited.

"Hush! Don't curse. You'll get skelped[1] if the Wobbs hear you." Herbert puts his hand on Jim's mouth. The "Wobbs" is a code word for the nuns that run the orphanage. Jim pushes Herbert's hand away.

"You can't leave! Where would you go?" asks Herbert skeptically.

"I'm being discharged. I'm leaving tomorrow morning with Father Murray to Inverness by train."

---

[1] smacked, beaten

"Discharged? So, you are truly leaving! What's in Inverness?" Jim signals Herbert to hold his tongue. Two Wobbs walk by and Jim and Herbert give a slight bow in respect.

"Come, come, come to the room," urges Jim. Once in Jim's room, which he shares with Herbert and two other fellow orphans, Jim pulls out from underneath his bed a green canvas duffle bag, opens the chest drawers, and starts pulling out his clothes.

"What are you doing?" utters Orville who barges into the room. Orville is a young lad from Birmingham and is one of the three roommates of Jim. Orville is the youngest of the four with eleven years of age.

"Jim is being discharged. He's leaving Thebes House tomorrow morning," replies Herbert.

"Where are you going?" questions Orville.

"Inverness," answers Jim while packing the bag.

"Inverness? Where is that?" asks Orville in a high pitch voice.

"Up north," answers Herbert. "Now, shut up. What are you going to do in Inverness? Are you going to another orphanage?" inquires Herbert curiously.

"Father Murray found me a job. I have no idea what for job, but anything else than this dreaded place is worth trying." The two roommates remain still. Jim pauses packing and smiles to the two mates.

"Come on lads, don't get all twinkly eyed on me. I'll write you regularly!" The two roommates smile but remain quiet. In their hearts they are glad for Jim. He is leaving this rotten place tomorrow and they wish that they could go with him.

"Do you trust Father Murray?" asks Herbert in a hushed voice.

"I have no choice. I'll have to if I ever want to leave this place." Herbert and Orville look at each other with an ominous face.

II

It's November the 2nd, 1950, five thirty in the morning. Jim swings his duffle bag and puts it on his right shoulder. He nods to his three roommates and quietly leaves the room. He said his goodbyes to his friends. On the way to the stairs Jim hears hushed and ghostly voices coming from behind the closed doors.

"Godspeed, Jim."

"Take care Jim."

"Write us Jim. Don't forget us." Word of his discharge has spread around. Nothing is a secret in the orphanage except for the real secrets. The whispered well-wishes of his fellow orphans are like muffled moans of chained souls longing for freedom. Jim knows the feeling. He has quietly wished many fellow discharged orphans Godspeed from behind the closed door of his room. The only feeling one has at such an occasion is one of hope mixed with helplessness. A hope that one day will be your turn to leave the choking hallways of Thebes House. That day has come for Jim. Although he has a heavy heart for leaving his yearlong friends, Jim can barely keep his excitement from openly showing. The walk down the stairs feels liberating. The foyer is scantly lit. Jim puts his duffle bag down and sits down on a wooden bench. It is cold and dark. The boy locks his eyes on the large crucifix with a nailed Jesus hanging on the far end wall of the hall. It is as if Jesus himself is asking Jim to please help him down and take him out of this place. Jim smiles and a sinister thought crosses his mind, *'if you're the son of the Almighty it should not be so difficult to hop off and just walk away'*. His eyes are fixed on Jesus' face. Motionless as if frozen in time Jesus hangs there day in and day out. The Wobbs demand from all orphans to make the sign of the cross every single time one passes in front of the dead Jesus hanging on the cross. Not doing the sign of the cross could get one punished. The Wobbs would say that not doing the sign will send one to hell where the punishment would be much harsher than the skelping we get here on Earth. Slowly Jim does the sign of the cross. Does Jesus really care? The hanging, bloody, and emaciated man on the cross doesn't budge. His eyes are glassy and hold a chilling stare as if looking into a void. "Why if you're so good and merciful you allow this dreadful place to exist" asks Jim to Jesus. As always, Jesus does not answer.

The large hallway door cracks open and the November chill invades the hall. Father Murray steps in.

"Evans!" bawls the priest loudly.

"Yes, Father, I'm ready," responds Jim. He stands up and grabs his bag. In the silence of the morning Jim steps outside. It is windy and cold. He takes a last glance at the dormitory windows on the first and second floors. Jim sees shadowy figures lurking behind the windows. Warm goodbyes are not allowed at Thebes House. All must transpire in silence and calm. "It is the way Jesus died on the cross, in silence and calm," say the Wobbs. No goodbyes, no farewells, no so longs, only silence and stillness is acceptable.

"Step in the car," utters Father Murray. The driver opens the rear door and Jim pushes the duffle bag in the car and takes his place on the back seat. Father Murray sits in front next to the driver. Cadbury Street is poorly lit, and the road looks somber and gloomy. The driver puts the car in gear, and they are on their way to the Aberdeen railway station. The car ride is somewhat bumpy and in complete silence. At the railway station the driver stops the car. Jim and Father Murray get out. The priest hands some money over to the driver who nods, steps into the car, and drives away. In the almost ten years that Jim resided in Thebes House he has been only once at the railway station. That was about six years ago when Archbishop Carlo visited the orphanage. All the orphans were bused to the train station, dressed in their best garments, and waving a small yellow and white flag. Jim remembers that day as if it was yesterday. "All smiles, all smiles," cheered the Wobbs when Archbishop Carlo stepped out of the station. "Wave your flag," commanded Mother Agnes. How hypocritical it all was recalls Jim.

Jim and Father Murray step onto the train. The boy has only been once before in a train and that was when his aunt in London accompanied him from London to Aberdeen to be interned at Thebes House. Jim never saw his aunt back again. The boy did not receive a single letter from his relatives in all of the ten years at Thebes House. He was just dumped here. The pain in Jim's heart for being deserted like a dog is very much present. He cannot, and will not, ever forgive her for doing that. The hate for his aunt fills his heart as much as the hate for Thebes House. Father

Murray and Jim take a seat in second class and within a few minutes the train starts moving and a sharp whistle makes the boy jump up in his seat. The clack-clog sound of the tracks slowly starts to get faster paced. Jim peers out of the window. '*Goodbye Aberdeen.*' The city is still cloaked in darkness. Only the scant street lights and some dimly lit buildings are visible as the train moves out of the city.

"Father?" utters Jim in a low voice.

"Yes, my son?"

"What am I going to do in Inverness?" asks Jim shyly.

"You're going to take a boat to the North, to the town of John o' Groats where you'll meet your employer," answers Father Murray somewhat cheerful.

"What am I going to do there, Father?"

"There you'll meet Mr. Shaw the Principal Lighthouse Keeper of the lighthouse on the island of Muckle Skerry. You'll be his apprentice and take over his duties when he retires."

"What is a lighthouse?" asks Jim.

"It's a tall tower with a very bright light on top of it and located on the seashore. It's there for ships to see at night and in foul weather so they don't run into the cliffs."

"What does a lighthouse keeper do?" inquires Jim in a somewhat anxious tone of voice.

"He keeps the light on and maintains the lighthouse in good condition, a noble job lad. Now keep quiet, will you?" Father Murray opens a book, puts his spectacles on, and concentrates on reading. Jim leans back and his heart shrinks. '*Lighthouse keeper, what kind of a job is that?*' '*Where is this island Muckle Skerry?*' The clack-clog rhythmic sound of the tracks has a lulling effect on the senses. Jim closes his eyes and goes into some sort of introspection.

'*I don't want to be a lighthouse keeper! I don't want to live on an island! I want to travel and see more of the world. I want to go to India and Australia. I want to fare the seas. What's so noble in keeping a stupid light on? Why me? Send the Thebes House hanging Jesus to tend the light! Why me? Where is this Muckle Skerry? What kind of people lives there? What kind of man is this Mr. Shaw?'* Slowly a feeling of anxiety creeps into Jim. The train to Inverness rides on.

III

"Tickets please!" blurts the conductor. Jim spirals out of a slumber. Father Murray produces two tickets out of his satchel. The conductor takes them, looks at the tickets, clips them, and hand the tickets back over to Father Murray.

"Inverness in twenty minutes!" the uniformed man hollers and continues his way down the wagon asking the passengers for their tickets. The sun is shining now. There is a reddish glow in the sky. What a beautiful landscape. The Scottish Highlands shimmer in the reddish radiance. Jim clings to the window savoring the spectacular sight of the hilly land in the morning light.

"Isn't that a sight?" asks Father Murray.

"Yes, Father, it's wonderful."

"God has His ways of filling the spirit with joy and this is one of them," whispers Father Murray. Jim sits back straight in his seat. *'It's the sun that does this. God has nothing to do with it'* contemplates Jim irritated. The train whistle utters a pair of sharp shrieks. The clanging of a bell runs by. Father Murray stares out of the window and with a voice full of reverence utters, "it's the way God reveals His presence to us mere mortals." Jim looks down to the floor and frowns. "Hypocrite," mutters Jim inaudibly.

About fifteen minutes later the train noticeably slows down and starts an elaborate dance of changing tracks. The bumping and screeching sound of the wheels on the tracks creeps up Jim's spine. As the train negotiates the tracks, the boy sees at a distance the spire of a church. It's a cold but sunny day. It's a wonderful day. Finally, the train arrives at Inverness railway station and stops. Father Murray and Jim quickly make their way out of the railway station.

"Stay here," orders Father Murray. Jim puts his duffle bag on the floor next to the Cameron Highlanders monument located at the station's entrance. Father Murray walks over to a car and talks to the driver. He shuffles in his satchel and hands the driver something.

"Come Jim! We have a ride to the quay!" hollers Father Murray. The boy grabs his duffle bag and hurries over to Father Murray. The driver opens the car trunk and Jim puts the bag in it. They step into the car.

"To the ferries, right Father?" asks the driver in a heavy Scottish slang.

"Yes, the John o' Groats ferryboat," replies the priest.

"The Groats, what yer[2] gaunnae[3] dae[4] there? They all Christians there!" chuckles the driver. Father Murray gazes at the driver.

"The lad got a job there," answers the priest.

"A job in Groats? Och, there's only farms there. What a young lad like him gaunnae dae there?" sniggers the driver.

"Do what God assigned him to do," replies Father Murray dryly. The driver looks at the priest. Father Murray's eyes are stone cold. The driver shuts up and drives on. Once at the quay, the

---

[2] your
[3] going to
[4] do

driver stops the car, and everybody gets out. Jim fetches his bag from the car trunk. The blabbermouth driver gives Jim a pat on the shoulder.

"Good luck, laddie, hope yer work keeps ye hoachin'," says the driver. He shakes the priest's hand, steps in the car, and speeds away.

"Hoachin'?" asks Jim to Father Murray.

"That means 'busy' my son," replies the priest. Although Jim lived in Aberdeen for almost ten years, his contact with the common Scot was scarce. The Scottish slang was not very much used at the orphanage. The language was considered disrespectful and brutish by the Wobbs. Jim and Father Murray walk over to the quay and stop at the gangway to the ferryboat.

"Now, my son, here we must part ways. Take this to keep you safe and to help you on the way." Father Murray takes Jim's hand and puts a crucifix and two one-pound notes in it. The boy remains silent.

"Mr. Shaw will be waiting for you at the pier of John o' Groats. Show him the crucifix and he'll know it's you. Do your prayers, Jimmy, and may God be with you." Father Murray and Jim shake hands and the priest walks away without a single glance back. Although the sun is bright, there is a cold stingy wind from the west. The horrible feeling of being dumped surfaces again. Father Murray didn't show a twitch of emotion. He did what he had to do and now he will probably head back to Aberdeen. Jim puts the crucifix and the one-pound notes in his pocket, picks up his bag, and boards the ferryboat.

"Excuse me Sir," asks Jim to a middle-aged man standing on the deck.

"Is this the ferry to John o' Groats?" The man looks at Jim and smiles.

"Yes, it is, laddie," he responds cheerful.

"Are ye going to the Groats?" asks the man.

"Yes, I am," answers Jim. "I live in Groats. I am Harris McLeod, but everybody calls me Harry. Who are ye?" Jim puts down his bag and answers,

"I am Jim Evans from Aberdeen."

"Ye don't sound Aberdeen, laddie."

"I was born in London but moved to Aberdeen at the beginning of the war."

"Och, a Sassenach[5]! No wonder. What takes ye to Groats?" Harry lights his pipe.

"I'm to be the apprentice lighthouse keeper on an island called Muckle Skerry."

"Ye're to go to Muckle Skerry? There's nothing out there young man but wind, rain, cold, grass, birds, rocks, and Crazy Lew!" chortles the man.

"Crazy Lew?" asks Jim anxiously.

"Aye! He's the lighthouse keeper on Muckle Skerry. Strange old man he is: sort of a hermit. I see him once in a while in Groats doing the messages[6]. He speaks to no one. He buys his supplies, steps on his boat, and vanishes out to sea. He's not seen for weeks; strange lad he is this Crazy Lew." Jim gets the shivers. Is this Crazy Lew the man Father Murray called Mr. Shaw?

"Uhm, excuse me Sir, but is this man, Crazy Lew, last named Shaw?"

"I think he is laddie. I think his name is Lewis Shaw. Strange fellow he is: somewhat creepy I must say." The ferryboat's horn gives a few short blows and the boat starts moving away from the quay. Jim pulls out the crucifix from his pocket. He looks at it and unnoticed by anyone flips it overboard. If this is God's assignment, he won't need it. A horrible feeling of loneliness rushes

---

[5] Scottish slang for Englishman
[6] "doing the messages" is slang for buying provisions

into his heart. '*Why am I on this boat*', asks Jim to himself. He could step off at the next stop and just disappear. But the boy knows that with only two pounds in his pocket he won't make it very far. A cloak of fear envelopes him. Mixed with the fear, rises a boil of anger. He is dumped again for the second time in his life. For months there were persistent rumors at the Thebes House that the Wobbs wanted to purge the teens, boys and girls, fifteen years and older.

"I guess we've seen too much and have become more resistant to the Wobbs" utters Jim in a low voice.

"Now is the time to make us disappear into the nothing" murmurs Jim. Slowly the boat makes its way out of the river Ness and into Moray Firth. The waters are calm. The journey to Muckle Skerry and to meet Crazy Lew is on.

IV

Before reaching John o' Groats, the ferryboat makes stops at the towns of Helmsdale and Wick. Jim arrives at John o' Groats harbor at approximately three o' clock in the afternoon. The wind and seas have picked up a bit and the ferryboat rolls more noticeably over the waves when arriving at John o' Groats. The boat is moored, and the gangway slid out.

"Hey laddie," hollers Harry.

Courtesy of the Muckle Skerry Archives at The John o' Groats Foundation.

"There he is auld boy; Crazy Lew is waiting for ye." Harry slaps Jim on the back and goes down the gangway onto the pier. Jim's heart pounds fast. The man on the pier is about six feet tall, well built, and of a somewhat fierce appearance. Jim feels as if he's glued to the ferryboat deck. The man has a white beard and short white hair on his head. He's dressed in an impermeable seafarer's coat with a long grey shawl around his neck. He has a pipe in his mouth and his hands in his coat's pockets. The old man looks menacing. Slowly, Jim musters the courage to pick up his bag and drag himself down the gangway onto the pier. The day turns grey and cloudy. The sunny weather of that morning in Inverness is all but gone. Each step Jim takes feels like as if he is dragging a huge boulder on a chain. The big old man fixes his eyes on the boy. The boy stops a couple of yards away from the man and puts down the duffle bag.

"Mr. Shaw?" asks Jim in a low voice. The man takes a short step towards Jim, takes the pipe out of his mouth, and asks, "Mr. Evans?"

"Yes, yes, Sir. James Evans from the Thebes House in Aberdeen."

"Show me the crucifix," mumbles the old man in a throaty voice.

"It, it, it fell overboard sir during the crossing on the ferryboat." The old man's gaze does not flinch. Jim stands there as if petrified.

"Aye, I'm Lewis Shaw, Principal Lighthouse Keeper of Muckle Skerry. Now, let's gau before it turns dark." The old man turns and motions Jim to follow him. He walks with a notable limp on his right leg. However, his appearance is impressive. The old man does not seem someone to mess with. They walk some thirty yards down the pier and stop.

"Hand me yer bag," utters Shaw. Jim gives it to him. With a swift motion Shaw flings the duffle bag on board of a boat called 'Hope'. It is about fifty-five feet long and has a single mast.

"Hop on," murmurs Shaw. The boy does so followed by the old man. Shaw opens the door of the aft cabin and goes inside. A few seconds later the deep sound of an engine is heard, and black smoke appears at the rear of the boat. The boat deck vibrates in synch with the roar of the engine. Shaw gets out of the cabin, steps onto the pier, and unties the moorings. He steps back on the boat, pulls in the plank, and limps over to the helm. He motions the boy to sit down on the deck.

It took approximately thirty minutes to make the crossing to Muckle Skerry. It was the longest thirty minutes in Jim's life. The sea is choppy and Hope rolls over the waves incessantly. Compared to the ferryboat, Hope is a nutshell. The nausea has the boy turning blue. He couldn't control the vomiting. His jacket and pants are smeared in puke. To top things off, rain starts pouring down and the wind picks up considerably. Once at the island, Shaw maneuvers the boat to get close to what seems to be two massive wooden poles sticking out of the sea. Skillfully he hobbles over to the bow and ties the boat to one of the poles with a thick and massive rope. He does the same at the stern. Shaw unties the sloop named 'Cheers', hanging at the boat's stern, and slowly lowers it into the water. The old man picks up Jim's duffle bag and throws it into the sloop. Shaw grabs a rope and handily steps over the boat railing and boards the sloop. Jim stands at the stern and stares at the bobbing sloop.

"Come on lad, we ain't got all day!" hollers Shaw. The boy grabs the rope and cautiously puts his right leg over the boat railing. His legs are all jellied up. Hope and the sloop bob up and down as if purposely trying to throw him into the sea. Slowly the boy lowers himself into the sloop.

"See Evans, all well. Start getting used to it ma boy!" hollers Shaw in a throaty voice. He fixes the ores and rows the sloop into a cove. They reach the shore and step out of the sloop. Jim winces; the water is freezing. Shaw pulls 'Cheers' out of the water and drags it to the deep end of the cove where there is something like a small crane sticking out on top of the cliff. He hooks the sloop on chains hanging from the crane and climbs up a concrete stair to the top of the cliff. Shaw motions the boy to follow him. Although there is still a low hanging sun, the skies are grey and dark. The boy reaches the top of the concrete stairs and drops his duffle bag to the ground. He can't believe his eyes. Harris was right! There is truly nothing here but rocks, grass, birds, and the lighthouse. There is not a single tree on the island. The light on the tower is lit and Jim watches somewhat in awe and horror at the rotating light beam emanating from the tower. The cold wind chills him to the bones. Shaw finishes hoisting up the sloop and taps the boy on the shoulder.

"Well, here we are, lad, Muckle Skerry. Isn't she bonnie[7]?" utters Shaw in an upbeat tone. Jim remains frozen. The old man picks up the boy's bag and starts walking to the lighthouse complex. The boy follows him hesitantly. The lighthouse complex consists of two towers; the tallest one has the light and the other has no light. The towers stand opposite each other some hundred feet apart and are oriented north to south. The lighthouse is the northern tower and the shorter one the southern tower; siding the towers are a string of cottages forming an inner courtyard. Everything is colored white. Shaw opens the door of the largest cottage house and steps inside. Jim hesitantly follows. The room is a combination of living room, dining room, and kitchen: all in one. The wooden beams supporting the roof are massive and in plain sight. Shaw drops the bag on the round table located at the center of the room. He lights two petrol lamps and limps over to a black heating stove in the corner. The old man shoves some straw and paper in it, lights it up, opens a wooden chest, with a brass hand shovel scoops some coal lumps, and shoves them into the stove. Shaw then inspects the chimney valve to make certain it's open.

---

[7] beautiful

"Always check the lum[8]. A closed lum can kill ye," utters Shaw and sits down at the table. He takes out his pipe, packs in tobacco, and lights it. Jim just stands there as if trapped in a horrid dream.

"Ye see that door there?" asks Shaw. Jim nods.

"That's yer room. Go and put on some dry clothes before ye catch a wheeze." The boy nods again, grabs his bag, and steps into the room. It is a small and somewhat stuffy room. There is a slender bed, a small desk, and a corner closet. However, there are no lamps in the room. Jim opens the door and steps back into the main room.

"Excuse me Sir, there are no lamps in the room," utters Jim in a shy and low voice.

"Och, aye, aye, Ah forgot to fetch the lamps." Shaw stands up, opens a cupboard in the kitchen and retrieves two petrol lamps. He fills them with kerosene and lights them.

"Here ye go, lad. Now, be careful, fire is a treacherous thing." Shaw hands the lamps over to Jim. A few minutes later the boy reappears in the main room wearing dry clothes. Shaw took off his seaman's coat and scarf and has a wooly vest and thick wooly pants on.

"Now, sit down lad. There are a few things ye need to know." Shaw motions Jim to take a seat at the table. The boy sits down. The old man pours him a cup of coffee.

"I know what's gaun on in yer mind. What a desolate place this is ye think. Well, it can get kind of lonely and spooky sometimes, but there are many fine things to dae around. Work starts every day at six in the morning. Breakfast is at five thirty. At noon time there is a thirty minutes break and work ends at six in the evening. On Sundays we rest; it's the Lord's Day. The first

---

[8] chimney

thing ye dae in the morning is to make up yer bed. Dinnae[9] let me catch yer bed all tossed up. On Saturdays we dae the regular house chores. Ye're a Christian son?" Jim hesitantly nods.

"Gaud[10]! So ye know yer prayers." The boy remains silent.

"Drink yer coffee before it gets cold," urges Shaw.

"I don't drink coffee, Sir," answers Jim softly. Shaw stands up and walks over to the stove. He shoves more coal in it.

"Don't call me sir. This ain't the army ye know. Call me Mr. Shaw; that will dae alright."

"Yes, Mr. Shaw," replies Jim.

"Ye dinnae sound Aberdeen, lad," states Shaw while pouring another cup of coffee for himself.

"I'm originally from London, Mr. Shaw."

"Och, a Sassenach! What ye doing at the Thebes House?"

"Both my parents died during the war. I was sent to the orphanage by my aunt."

"So sorry to hear that, ma lad. Horrible thing war," utters Shaw softly. The room goes quiet for a few minutes.

"Now, ye see that door over there?" asks the old man. Jim nods.

"That's ma quarters. Ye can roam everywhere around the lighthouse compound except in ma quarters, get that?" Jim quietly nods again.

"Gaud! Now put this on. Ah[11] have some friends to present ye." Shaw tosses a heavy canvas trench coat to Jim and puts on his impermeable.

"Follow me lad." Shaw fetches a lantern and steps outside. The rain has stopped, and darkness fell upon Muckle Skerry. The wind calmed down, but the cold persists. The two men walk across

---

[9] don't
[10] good
[11] First person singular "I"

the courtyard to the other side of the compound. Shaw slides opens a large wooden door. It's the barn.

"Hullo Margarethe, did ye miss me?" chuckles the old man. A black and white cow utters a loud moo.

"Och, Maggy, haud yer wheesht[12]! We have a new lad, here Mr. Evans." The cow moos again. There are four sheep, a bunch of chickens, and two pigs. The barn has a sharp odor, but it generally looks well in order.

"This is yer first order tomorrow, lad, barn duty," bawls Shaw loudly. Jim keeps a stoic face.

"I'll show ye what to dae tomorrow. Now, follow me." They step outside and Shaw closes the barn door. The beam of light from the lighthouse revolves and pierces the night like a hot knife in butter. The dark landscape and the revolving light beam give Jim an outer worldly and eerie feeling. They cross the courtyard and halt at the foot of the main tower. Shaw pulls the boy closer to him and looks up to the top of the tower. A wispy zooming sound fills the air.

"See that lad? That's the light. That's the sole reason we're here. Keep that always in mind. No matter what, rain, sleet, snow, or hail, the light is lit every night and in misty or foul weather. It's our first and foremost duty." Shaw's penetrating gaze pierces Jim.

"Ye follow lad?" asks the old man sharply.

"Yes, Mr. Shaw I follow," replies the boy in a low voice.

"Gaud! Now, let's get back in and fetch some dinner, shall we?" Shaw limps back to the main cottage. The zooming sound has a hypnotic effect on Jim.

"What am I doing here?" whispers Jim. The boy stares at the light. Swirl and swirl it does. Suddenly Jim is startled by a sharp whistle.

---

[12] hold your quiet, shut up

"Come on, lad!" hollers Shaw from the cottage door. Like engulfed in a dream Jim slowly walks back to the cottage. He steps inside and Shaw closes the door.

V

Weeks go by and Jim is assigned only housekeeping duties: barn duty, water duty, paint duty. But the worst of all chores is can-duty which is an everyday responsibility of Jim. Can-duty entails the cleaning and washing of the shit-bucket located in the shit-shack at the far corner of the complex. Every evening before supper the excrement in the can has to be discarded and the bucket and shit-shack cleaned. Jim is trying hard, but things are not working out.

Every morning before breakfast Shaw inspects Jim's bed. One morning Jim oversleeps and the old man barges in. The boy jumps out of bed in a hurry. Without saying a word, Shaw pulls the mattress off the bed, rips the sheets apart, and throws them around the room. All Shaw says is "sow the pieces and tidy yer bed." Jim is furious but manages to maintain his composure. Shaw gives the boy a brief tour in the lighthouse but does not show him how it works. When Jim asks what this is, or what does that do, Shaw answers coldly "yer not ready yet for that." For now, all the boy is good for is to do mundane house stuff. The tension between the two is reaching a boiling point.

December 24th, 1950, Christmas Eve, 7:00 PM. Shaw made Scotch broth for dinner. It's a welcome change in menu. Jim is sick of the tatties and colcannon. Shaw retrieves the soup pan from the cooking hearth and places it on the round table. The broth smells wonderful and its vapor fill the room. It snowed a little today and the wind is strong. The temperature outside is below freezing.

"Did ye wash yer hands?" asks Shaw.

"Yes Mr. Shaw," answers Jim sternly. Shaw serves two big scoops of broth in the boy's plate.

"There is no work tomorrow, except for the light and the can," utters Shaw in a raspy voice.

"Tomorrow we honor Jesus' birthday! Did ye dae the can?" inquires Shaw.

"No!" answers Jim resolutely. The old man freezes in place. He puts down the soup dipper, picks up Jim's soup plate and pours the broth back into the pot. Demonstratively Shaw puts the empty soup plate in front of the boy.

"Gau dae the can!" orders Shaw. Jim doesn't budge.

"Are ye deaf, lad? Gau dae the can Ah said!" bawls the old man. The boy doesn't move. Shaw hangs the broth pot in the hearth and sits down.

"What's in yer heid[13]?" asks Shaw in a somewhat defiant tone of voice.

"I won't clean the can. I'm sick of cleaning the can. I'm sick of this place. I don't want to be a lighthouse keeper. I just want to leave." The frustration and anger is palpable in Jim's voice. A muffled thump is heard, and the table trembles a little.

"Ye hear that?" asks Shaw with a broad smile on his face. The boy freezes up in his chair. He has never heard that sound before or felt the table shake like that.

"The swells," mumbles the old man in a low voice.

"Swells?" inquires Jim worried.

---

[13] head

"Huge waves. They come into Hell's Mouth from the west. They swell to considerable heights due to the narrows. Nobody leaves or comes to the Skerries tonight, too dangerous. There must be a storm brooding out there." Another muffled thump is heard, and the shakes are palpable.

"She's just like ye tonight; she's angry!" utters Shaw.

"She?" asks Jim.

"The sea lad, she has a temper. When she's mad ye dinnae mess with her 'cause she'll kill ye." *These must be huge waves to sound and shake the island like that* ponders the boy. The empty plate attracts Jim's attention. Shaw's eyes are fixed on him. The old man has a fixed grin on his face. The boy stands up, grabs the trench coat, and steps outside into the dark windy night. Briskly Jim crosses the inner courtyard in the direction of the shit-shack. He opens the door, enters, grabs the bucket from underneath the stool, walks to the outer yard wall, and empties the bucket. He pulls his scarf over his nose. Even though the excrement is frozen it still reeks. Jim throws the metal can on the ground and smashes it with a brick size rock until the bucket is flat like a pancake.

"Are ye done?" utters a calm voice behind Jim. It's Shaw standing there with a brand-new metal bucket in hand. Jim looks at him in disbelieve.

"Ah thought we need a new one any way," says Shaw in a sarcastic tone. He hands the boy the new bucket and points a finger in the direction of the shit-shack. Jim just stands there looking at Shaw, can in hand in the howling wind.

"On yer way, lad," insists Shaw.

"Dinnae smash this can, or we have to crap over the cliff." Shaw turns and heads back to the main cottage. Thump! Another swell hits and Jim sees the huge white misty foam splash over the cliff edge.

"I must get out of here," he whispers. Freezing raindrops start coming down. Jim hurries back to the shit-shack.

Twenty minutes later Jim enters the main cottage. It still rains and his trench coat is soaked. He takes it off, hangs it, and approaches the black stove to warm up. Shaw sits quietly at the table smoking his pipe.

"Did ye wash yer hands?" asks the old man.

"Yes, Mr. Shaw."

"Gaud! Now sit doon, let's eat." Shaw stands up, grabs the soup pot from the cooking hearth, puts it on the table, and serves two big scoops of Scotch broth to Jim. He scoops for himself, hangs the pot in the hearth, and takes a seat.

"Let's pray lad." In his usual everyday manner, Shaw brings his hands together and closes his eyes. Jim, still angry, doesn't budge.

"The Lord is ma Light and salvation — whom shall Ah fear? The Lord is the stronghold of ma life — of whom shall Ah be afraid? One thing Ah ask from the Lord, this only Ah seek: that Ah may dwell in the house of the Lord all the days of ma life, to gaze on the beauty of the Lord and to seek him in his temple. Thank ye Lord for our meal tonight. Amen."

"Amen," whispers Jim. Shaw picks up his spoon and starts to eat the broth. Jim doesn't move. Shaw looks at him and puts the spoon down.

"What?" asks Shaw.

"You really believe that stuff, don't you Mr. Shaw?" asks Jim while peering at the old man.

"Believe what stuff?" asks Shaw sternly.

"That the Lord will protect us. That we shall dwell in his house, and all of that," replies Jim.

"Why? Dinnae ye?" asks Shaw in a raspy voice. Jim hesitates for a moment. Shaw smiles, grabs his spoon, and resumes his meal.

"No," utters Jim in a low voice.

"I don't believe in it," iterates the boy. Shaw pauses for a moment and then resumes eating the broth without saying a word. Jim picks up the spoon and slowly scoops the broth. The wind howls fierce outside. Another thump is heard. The loud clatter of the rain against the windows fills the room with a strange echo as if a thousand birds are pecking on the glass panes.

Jim's mind wanders back in time to Christmas Eve 1946. It snowed in Aberdeen and the play yard of Thebes House has about two inches of fresh snow on it. Herbert and Jim ask Sister Mary if they may go out and play in the snow. It is six thirty in the evening, just after dinner. It is dark, but the yard lights are on. Sister Mary is one of the nicer Wobbs. She is young and has a pretty face. She thinks for a moment, smiles, and nods. "Just five minutes," she says, and she opens the door to the yard. Herbert and Jim storm outside.

"Shhht!" orders Sister Mary. If Mother finds out, we and Sister Mary will be in trouble. After a couple of minutes in the yard, Jim sees a tall figure approach Sister Mary in the doorway. It's Father Murray. He whispers something to Sister Mary, turns, and leaves. Immediately, Sister Mary calls Herbert and Jim in.

"Go to your room now," she commands.

"Are we in trouble, Sister?" asks Jim anxiously. Sister Mary is visibly nervous. She forces a smile and prompts the boys to go upstairs to the room. What happened that night, Jim wants to forget, but can't.

"Ye're not eating, lad. Broth gets cauld" prompts Shaw. Jim remains silent.

"Eat yer broth, it's gaud far ye!" The boy eats a spoon of broth. It's good. Mr. Shaw knows his cooking when he puts effort into it. However, it's usually potatoes, cauliflower, spinach, colcannon, or shortbread with crowdie. It starts to get on your nerves. Jim finishes the broth.

"There is mair[14] ye know!" utters Shaw and points his spoon to the pot. The boy shakes his head, takes his plate and spoon, and washes them in the washbowl in the kitchen.

"Ye're too young to be so sad, ma lad," says Shaw in a calm voice while eating the broth. Jim dries the plate and spoon and puts them in the kitchen cupboard. Shaw peers at the boy while munching the broth.

"Ye have great anger in ye. That's not gaud. It will consume ye from within. Ye've been jittery for days now: restless, irritated, like a caged dug[15]. Ah dinnae ken[16] what it is, but it ain't gaud." Shaw scoops a spoon of broth.

"I don't want to be here. Don't you understand that Mr. Shaw? It's that simple," retorts Jim in a firm voice.

"Och, neay, ma lad, Ah dae understand. Ah understand more than ye think. It is the anger ye carry inside that I dinnae understand. It's way bigger than merely a yearning to leave. It's a fester in ye." A chill creeps up Jim's spine. Shaw's tone of voice is calm but carries a strange echo of wisdom with it. He has never addressed Jim in that way before. He's never been this candid. The boy says goodnight and heads to his room. Shaw grabs his arm.

"The Lord ain't yer foe, ma lad. Learn to see. The swells out there are dangerous, yet bonnie! Ye don't mess with the swells. Ye don't mess with the Lord." Shaw lets go of Jim's arm. The boy retires to his room.

---

[14] more
[15] dog
[16] "I don't know"

VI

The main entrance hall of Thebes House is scantily lit as always. The moldy odor is penetrating. In front of the large crucifix with Jesus is a long oak table with about a dozen lit candles on it. Jim has his sight fixed on dead Jesus' face. Slowly he approaches the oak table to get a better look at the glassy stare of the son of God. The empty gaze of the effigy gives Jim the creeps. Slowly he does the sign of the cross and leans forward to get an even better look at the dead Jesus face. Suddenly, Jesus turns his head and looks Jim straight in the eyes, "don't mess with the swells," he groans.

Jim jumps up in bed all sweaty and panting. It's a dream, a nightmare. Muckle Skerry is veiled in darkness and the wind howls in an eerie high pitch. The roof cracks under the stress imposed by the wind. Jim lights a petrol lamp and puts his pants and vest on. He grabs the lamp and slowly cracks open the door to the main room. The main room is filled with the smell of a blend of pipe tobacco, coffee, and porridge. The old man sits at the table reading a book and a cup of coffee in his hand.

"Morning lad, sleep well?" The boy pulls a chair and sits down at the round table.

"Merry Christmas, lad. Porridge?" asks Shaw in an upbeat tone of voice.

"Merry Christmas, Mr. Shaw," answers Jim in a barely audible voice and nods. Shaw stands up, grabs a bowl, and fills it with steaming porridge. He puts the bowl and spoon in front of Jim who picks up the spoon and digs into the porridge.

"Hold on, laddie, say yer prayers." Jim frowns, puts down the spoon, and stoically utters "amen." He picks up the spoon and starts eating the porridge. Shaw sits down and lights the pipe.

"Dae ye know the story of the birth of Jesus?" asks Shaw loudly.

"Who doesn't," answers Jim laconically.

"From where are the three wise men?" probes the old man while taking a drag on the pipe.

"Persia, they say," replies Jim with a mouth full of porridge.

"Gaud! Ye know yer stuff! What did the three men bring for baby Jesus?"

"Myrrh, gold, and frankincense," responds the boy immediately.

"What are their names?" asks Shaw in a pushy tone.

"John, Jack, and Joe," utters Jim sarcastically. Shaw remains quiet and with a penetrating stare on Jim.

"You don't believe in that fairy tale, do you, Mr. Shaw?"

"How dae ye know it's a fairy tale?"

"How do you know it's not?" retorts Jim. Shaw remains quiet and stands up. He grabs his overcoat and puts it on.

"Belief and knowledge are different things. Now, grab yer gear. We must check the light." Shaw grabs a lantern and steps outside. Jim grabs the canvas trench coat and follows.

The wind is strong and the cold cuts through the bones. The old man limps in double pace to the lighthouse. He opens the door and both men get inside. The zooming sound turns into a steady hum. Jim takes a look at the spiral stair going up to the top: a swirl of steps that appear to have no end. As they approach the top of the tower, the humming steadily turns louder. They reach the top of the spiral stairs. Before Shaw opens the door to the light room, he warns Jim, "dinnae look straight into the light. It damages yer eyes." Jim nods. Shaw swings the door open and the light beam rushes by. The heat of the light is palpable. The low pitch hum is quite loud now. Jim puts his hand in front of his eyes and peers into the light in an attempt to see the lamp, a strange brass contraption with what looks like three big burning light bulbs on it. Shaw whacks Jim on the head.

"Dinnae dae that!" he orders. Circulating the lamp is a tall convex mirror that focuses the light into a beam. The mirror rotates around the lamp while attached to a circular rail. On the east side of the lamp is a metal gadget the size of a potato crate from which a rotating shaft drives a gear. The metal 'potato box' is driven by something that looks like an oversized bicycle chain coming from a side chamber. Shaw carefully inspects the railing on which the mirror rotates and afterwards directs his attention to the metal 'potato box'. He motions Jim to come closer.

"Pass me that rag!" hollers Shaw. The loud low pitch hum makes the old man's voice barely audible. Shaw points to the hanging rag. Jim picks it up and hands it over to Shaw. The old man retrieves a metal dipstick out of the 'potato box', looks at it, cleans it and slides the stick back into the box. A couple of seconds later he pulls the stick out again and looks at it. He motions the boy to come closer.

"See that? The oil edge must be between these lines: not above and not below. Ye follow?" Jim nods. The stick goes back in the metal box and Shaw steps over to a small door and opens it. The hum turns into a loud hammering sound. Inside the little room is the driving engine on a concrete block and beside it lays a horizontal metal cylindrical tank. Shaw steps into the little engine room and motions Jim to follow him. There is barely room for the two men. Shaw taps his finger on a gauge glass on the side of the tank. He closes the lower valve connecting the gauge glass and the tank and motions Jim to pass him a small brass cup lying on the floor. He puts the cup under the gauge glass drain and opens the drain valve. The oil drains out of the gauge. Shaw closes the drain and opens the valve connected to the tank. The oil immediately fills the gauge glass. The old man nods satisfied. He turns, puts two fingers on the engine block, and closes his eyes. After twenty seconds or so he removes his fingers and smiles. The old man doesn't say a word and motions Jim to get out of the engine room. Once outside, he shuts the engine room door. The loud hammering sound returns to a loud hum. Shaw grabs a pair of dark spectacles, puts it on, and looks straight into the light. He smiles again and points to the exit door. Once outside the light room, Shaw closes the door, takes the dark glasses off, and hangs them on a hook on the wall.

"She's doing gaud," utters the lighthouse keeper happily. Jim stands there brass cup in hand. Shaw takes a few steps down the spiral stairs and pauses in front of the window. The sun is rising, and a reddish glow fills the window.

"Here lad, look at that," says Shaw. Jim looks out of the window. The sight is unbelievable. The reddish sunlight accentuates the series of huge waves moving from west to east. The waves are colossal, the swells.

"Ain't that bonnie?" Jim remains still. The beauty of the sight is overwhelming. The two men look at the sight for a couple of minutes.

"Come on, lad, we ain't done yet," hollers Shaw. The boy jumps as if woken up from a dream. At his way down the stairs, Jim tries to catch a glimpse of that magnificent sight at each window looking eastward.

Once at the foot of the spiral stairs, Shaw opens a side door and steps in the room. Inside there is a large cubic metal tank and there is a wooden rack on the wall stacked with large petrol cans. Shaw takes the brass cup from Jim, opens a small lid on top of the metal tank, and pours the petrol in the tank.

"Nothing to waste," utters the old man and winks. He checks the tank's gauge glass in the same way as he did on that of the cylindrical tank upstairs.

"Got to check the gauges every week. Sometimes they clog up and give you false reading. That tricks you." He motions Jim to leave the room, closes the door, and readies his jacket to step outside in the freezing wind. They hurry back to the main cottage.

Once back inside the main cottage Shaw comments, "ain't she really devilish today?"

"The swells?" inquires Jim. "The wind!" rejoins Shaw.

"Howling like a bitch in heat yet cold like the hand of a corpse. Tell ye, lad, storm brooding!" He sits down, stuffs his pipe with tobacco, lights it and leans back.

"Now, tell me boy, what did Ah dae up there?" enquires Shaw sternly.

"Do what?" asks the boy.

"At the light, lad, the light! What did Ah dae?"

"You, you, checked the light, Mr. Shaw," utters Jim confused.

"Neay! What did I exactly dae! Tell me piece by piece what ye see me dae."

"I don't know what you did! I don't have a clue what's up there," snaps Jim irritated. Shaw leans forward and sharply gazes at Jim.

"Ah'm[17] not asking ye to tell me what's up there. Ah'm asking ye to tell me what ye saw me dae!" yells Shaw. Jim sours up and remains quiet.

"Well, lad? Cat got yer tongue?" mocks the old man.

"I don't know. I don't remember," utters Jim softly.

"Nonsense! Ye dae know what ye saw. Ye just refuse to say it." Jim stands up.

"I don't care what I saw because as soon as I get a chance I'm leaving this miserable place!" He hangs his trench coat and retires to his room. Shaw takes a drag on the pipe.

---

[17] "I am"

Jim spends the day in his room. At about five o'clock in the evening he reappears in the main area of the cottage. Shaw is cooking something, and it smells wonderful. The boy sits down at the round table.

"You inspected the rail of the mirror. Then, you checked the liquid level in the metal box," utters Jim in a low voice. Shaw stops stirring the cooking pot and faces Jim.

"The metal box is called a gearbox. Gau on," prompts Shaw.

"You drained the liquid from the glass tube of the round tank and refilled it. After that you put your fingers on the engine. I don't know what for. You also inspected the lamp using a pair of dark spectacles. Downstairs you checked the glass tube on the cubic metal tank." After reciting what Shaw did this morning in the lighthouse, Jim goes quiet. Shaw smiles and stands up. He limps over to a small bookcase located at the other end of the room. He browses around, pulls out a book, puts it on the table, and takes a seat.

"Ah know ye can read. What else did the nuns teach ye at Thebes House?" Jim shrugs shyly.

"Did ye get some mathematics?" asks the old man . Jim shrugs again.

"Did ye get arithmetic?" No answer from Jim.

"By the way, the glass tube is called a gauge glass. What color is the liquid in the gauge glass?"

"Clear yellow," replies Jim. Shaw picks up his pipe and lights it. The wind has calmed down considerably but it's raining again. The old man grabs the book, stands up, limps over to the bookcase, and returns it to its place.

"Ye're not ready yet for that," he mumbles.

"Ready for what?" inquires Jim sternly.

"Never mind, lad, now go do the can and dinnae forget to wash yer hands. Supper is almost ready."

"The can! The mop! The broom! The barn! The shit-shack! The water cistern! That's all I've been doing for weeks. You don't need an apprentice! You need a maid!" bawls Jim explosively. Shaw ignores him completely. The boy puts on the trench coat and goes outside.

After about thirty minutes Jim returns, hangs the petrol lamp, and takes off his coat.

"Did ye wash yer hands?" Jim nods and sits down.

"Gaud! Now, let's have some gaud auld Banach stew for Christmas!" utters Shaw excited.

"Banach stew?"

"Aye! Auld Banach stew. Auld Banach was the lighthouse keeper before me and was ma teacher. He's deid. He taught me all ah know about this place. He also taught me how to make Polish stew. The auld man was Polish. Ah dinnae ken how he stranded here at the Skerries. But he knew his stuff. He called the stew 'bigos'[18]. Here try it." Shaw puts a bowl of bigos in front of Jim. It smells delicious. The old man sits down and places his bowl of bigos on the table.

"Let's say our prayers, lad." Shaw folds his hands and closes his eyes.

"The Lord is ma shepherd; Ah shall not want. He maketh me lie down in green pastures: he leadeth me beside the still waters. He restoreth ma soul: he leadeth me in the paths of righteousness for his name sake. Surely goodness and mercy shall follow me all the days of my life: and Ah will dwell in the house of the Lord forever. Thank ye Lord for our daily meal. Amen."

"Amen," whispers Jim and immediately digs into the stew. It is fantastic! He has never eaten something so delicious: not even at the Thebes House. His sour demeanor changes immediately to a refreshed appearance. Shaw looks at him and smiles.

---

[18] A Polish stew

"Dae ye like it?" asks the old man. Jim nods vigorously with a mouth full of stew.

"This is our Christmas treat. Auld Banach always saved his stew for Christmas Day. It takes some work, but it's well worth it, dinnae ye think so?" Jim nods again.

"Ah thought maybe auld Banach stew will put a smile on yer face," chortles Shaw.

"Haven't seen ye smile since the day ye're here." Jim forces a smile with a mouth full. Shaw shakes his head and eats his stew.

After two full bowls of bigos, Jim and Shaw's bellies are stuffed. The boy washes the bowls and utensils, pours a glass of milk, and sits down. Shaw lights his pipe. The wind calmed down but it's still drizzling outside.

"Ye play chess, ma lad?" Jim shakes his head.

"Ye wanna learn how to play chess?" enquires Shaw in a low voice. The boy shrugs. The old man stands up and goes into his room. He reappears from the room with a wooden chess board and a wooden box. Shaw opens the box and pours the chess pieces on the board.

"Aren't they bonnie?" asks Shaw cheerfully.

"Bought it in Edinburgh many years ago." Jim remains quiet looking at the chess pieces.

"Ye're not much of a blether[19], aren't ye lad?" comments Shaw as he sets the pieces.

"Now, this piece is the king. It moves like this with only one square at a time." Shaw patiently goes through the motions of each of the pieces while also explaining their importance in the game. Jim listens and observes carefully without saying a word. After a half hour of instructions, they try their first game of chess. The night is quiet, no howling wind and no thumping swells. The night is spent playing quiet games of chess.

---

[19] talker

VII

It is late January 1951. Jim and Shaw are on their way to John o' Groats crossing Hell's Mouth on Shaw's boat named *Hope*. The day is cold but sunny, and the sea is smooth and tranquil. It's Saturday, market day in Groats. They need to resupply food and coal for the coming months. Shaw brought with him many empty jute sacks to put the provisions in. They moor Hope at the John o' Groats pier and walk into town. It's the first time Jim is back on the mainland since he arrived on Muckle Skerry. Shaw, carrying a bunch of empty jute sacks on his back, limps his way straight to the market square followed by Jim.

As they pass by, the town people keep staring at the two and hide their snickering with a hand in front of the mouth. A young mother with a child points a finger at Shaw and says to the kid "see, that's Crazy Lew I told ye about. If ye're not gaud, Crazy Lew will come far ye." The small kid turns and clasps the mother's leg in fear. Shaw doesn't utter a word and limps forward focused on reaching the market square. Once at the square, he directs himself immediately to a vegetable stall attended by an old lady. The old man stands in front of the stall and puts down the jute sacks.

"Hello Mr. Shaw. Ye look gaud. That time of year again, ain't it?" asks the old lady in a shrieky voice. Shaw nods and hands the woman a note and two jute sacks.

"Och, the usual Ah see." She smiles and disappears in the aft room of the stand. Jim looks around and notices the attention they attract from all in the square. The boy gets closer to Shaw and whispers, "everybody is looking at us." Shaw doesn't say a word. The old lady reappears from the aft room followed by a young lad carrying the two sacks: one filled with potatoes and the other with onions. He puts them on the floor next to Shaw and hurries back inside. The old man hands the woman a note and a few coins and motions Jim to pick up the sacks.

"Bring them to Hope and lock them in the cabin," orders Shaw. Jim does what he's told and in a wink of time he's back in the market square where Shaw is waiting for him with four sacks of coal. Each man grabs two sacks and start to head for Hope.

"Lewis Shaw is that ye?" hollers a voice in the market square. Shaw keeps limping his way forward without heeding the voice.

"Someone is calling you, Mr. Shaw," says Jim.

"Keep walking. No business with no one here," rebukes the old man with a groan.

"Shaw! It's McGraw, Robert McGraw, the Black Watch, dinnae ye remember me?" hollers the voice again. Shaw stops, puts the sacks down and turns. About forty feet away is an old man in a wheelchair. His legs are covered with a thick woolly blanket and he looks about the same age as Shaw. Lewis Shaw slowly limps over to the man.

"Ye old rat! I knew it was ye! It's me, Bob McGraw, 1st Battalion, Royal Scots. Dinnae ye remember?" Shaw stops in front of the seated man and fixes his gaze on the man's face as if trying to remember him. Slowly a smile appears on Shaw's face.

"Ma Lord, Bobbie McGraw, it's ye. What in the Lord's name are ye doing in John o' Groats?"

"Ah'm visiting a grandson of ma and to see ma newborn great-grandson. What are ye doing here?" asks the man.

"Ah'm the principal lighthouse keeper on Muckle Skerry. Ah'm doing the messages here with ma apprentice." Shaw waves Jim to come closer.

"This is Jim Evans, ma apprentice lighthouse keeper." Jim shakes hands with the wheel chaired man.

"What happened to ye, if Ah may ask," inquires Shaw and points to the man's legs.

"Poelcapelle," answers the man in a low voice and lifts the blanket. The man's legs are stumps. A chill creeps up Jim's spine. Shaw nods.

"Let's grab a pint, shall we? Catch up on things," utters the man cheerfully.

"Can't do, auld lad, have to load provisions and sail to the Skerry before dark; some other day, maybe." Shaw shakes hands with the man and signals Jim to move on. The chaired man smiles and says goodbye: "Gaud to see ye again Lewis." Shaw turns, smiles, and waves goodbye.

"What happened to the man? What happened to his legs?" asks Jim curiously. Shaw remains silent.

"What is 'Poelcapelle'?" inquires Jim anxiously. Shaw limps forward without uttering a word.

"Were you in the army?" Shaw stops, drops the sacks, and grabs Jim by the neck.

"Listen, ye wee Sassenach, shut yer geggie[20], will ye. Haud yer wheesht and move on!" bawls Shaw. He pushes Jim, grabs the sacks, and limps on.

At the boat, Shaw puts the provisions in the cabin, grabs two more jute sacks, and climbs back on the pier.

"Ye stay here. Be right back." The old man limps back to the market. Jim puts his hand on his throat. The old man has an

---

[20] mouth

iron grip. This is the first time Shaw gets aggressive on him. The seagulls squeal incessantly.

"What is a Sassenach?" whispers Jim. He steps onto the pier.

"I can just disappear now, flee this miserable place and never return," murmurs Jim. The old man wouldn't know where to look. The temptation to leave gets a hold on Jim. His mind is in turmoil. '*Leave, but where to*' he thinks. '*I haven't got a penny.*' An avalanche of despair engulfs the boy. He steps back on the boat and sits down next to the mast. '*What kind of man is Shaw? Nobody in Groats talks to him. Everybody sniggers behind his back. Mothers scare their children by mentioning him. What has he done to deserve that?*'

"Hey lad!" hollers Shaw standing on the pier with two sacks full of provisions.

"Here ye go!" Shaw throws the sacks for Jim to catch and the old man steps into the boat. He turns on the engine, unties the moorings, and slowly maneuvers Hope out of the harbor. Hell's Mouth is a little choppy but manageable. Shaw sets course to Muckle Skerry.

"Why do the people in Groats treat you this way?"

"Treat me what way?" asks Shaw in a raspy voice.

"They snigger at you behind your back. They call you Crazy Lew. What have you done to them?"

"Nothing. I just keep to maself. They live other people's lives. Gossip and innuendo, that's what they gaud at."

"Who is the man in the wheelchair?" Shaw doesn't answer. He taps the compass and sticks the pipe in his mouth.

"What is the Black Watch?" asks Jim sharply. Shaw gives no reaction.

They arrive at Muckle Skerry and manage to haul the jute sacks to the cottage. Shaw dumps the coal in the coal pit and commands Jim to take the other sacks to the provision room. The old man goes to the lighthouse and turns the light on. After a

'HOPE' by James McMurry. Courtesy of The Groats Museum.

considerable effort, Jim gets the rest of the sacks stored in the provision room. He closes the door and looks at the top of the tower. The light turns on. Jim's frustration wells up. *'What am I doing here? Why didn't I just vanish in Groats?'* He walks over to the main cottage and steps inside. A desperate feeling wells up in his heart like a spring with dark muddy waters. The boy crashes on a chair and stares blankly at the kitchen hearth. Shaw barges in, takes off his coat, and starts rummaging in the kitchen.

"Am I getting paid for this?" asks Jim.

"Aye, three pounds," answers Shaw.

"I haven't seen a penny yet," replies Jim sourly.

"That's because ye haven't produced anything yet," rebukes the old man immediately. Jim stands up.

"I've been doing all my chores!"

"Aye, chores, has to be done. On the light ye haven't done much," utters Shaw stoically.

"You haven't shown me what to do!"

"Ye haven't paid attention and shown little interest." Jim sits down and shuts up.

"Gau dae the can!" orders Shaw sternly. Barely containing his anger, Jim grabs his coat and leaves the cottage.

VIII

"Father forgive me for I've sinned," utters Jim in a low voice. The confessional[21] has a musky odor mixed with the usual moldy stench of Thebes House. The House's chapel is dark and filled with lit candles.

"Tell me, my son, what is so heavy on your soul?" inquires the priest.

"I have seen things Father that I shouldn't have seen, sinful things Father."

"What's so terrible my son?" asks the priest in a calm voice. Jim remains silent for a minute and the priest reassures Jim that his confessions are safe with him.

"Father, I, I saw Father Murray and Sister Mary in the library," says Jim cautiously.

"Go on my son." After a minute of silence Jim continues.

"They were doing bad things, Father; things that I shouldn't have seen."

"What were they doing son?"

---

[21] a wooden booth with two separate compartments used for holding confessions

"Sister Mary was...was...." Jim goes silent.

"Sister Mary was doing what son?"

"She was gobbling[22] Father Murray, Father." The priest remains still. After a minute or so the pastor asks, "are you certain of what you saw my son?"

"Yes Father."

"What time was it then my son?"

"About eleven o'clock at night, Father, on Christmas eve."

"What were you doing in the library at that time son?"

"I couldn't sleep Father." The priest remains quiet for a few minutes.

"Don't tell anyone about this. Do twenty Our Lord's Prayer. Don't tell anyone. God will take care of this."

Jim does the sign of the cross and leaves the confessional.

Two days after Jim's confession, Father Murray appears at the boy's room after lunch.

"Evans, you come with me," orders the priest. Jim hesitantly follows the pastor. Father Murray stops at a heavy wooden door, unlocks it, and grabs Jim's arm ushering him to step inside. Jim's heart beats fast and uncontrollable. The hallway is dark, and the moldy odor is worse than ever. Jim has never been in this part of Thebes House.

"Keep walking," commands Father Murray. The hallway is sloped downward as if going underground. The priest puts a hand on Jim's shoulder as a sign to stop. Father Murray unlocks and opens a second door, grabs Jim by the arm and shoves him in the dark room. The boy is intensely scared. The pastor lights two candles and takes off his robe. Jim squats down in a corner.

"Ye wee[23] bastart rat! Spying on me at night, aren't ye?!" yells the priest.

---

[22] blowjob

"Oh no, no, Father, I couldn't sleep," cries Jim. From the inner pocket of his robe, Murray produces a meter-long bamboo cane. He grabs Jim by the hair and violently drags him to a chair where he ties him up with his chest to the back of the chair and rips open Jim's shirt. Jim cries and begs for mercy but at no avail. No cry from the catacombs reaches the ears of the Wobbs of Thebes House; they don't want to hear it.

"I'll give you fifteen lashes for not being in your room when you had to and for spying and telling lies in confession!" hollers Father Murray.

"If you dare to continue telling those lies to anyone, I assure ye that fifty more lashes will be coming to ye!" The bamboo cane makes a swooshing sound and a fleshy dry whipping thud is heard. Jim bites his lip to try to absorb the pain. His back feels as if on fire. His eyes get dark and he loses consciousness.

"Damn!" shouts Jim. He dozed off sitting on the stool in the shit-shack. The shit-shack is about the same size as the compartment of the confessional. The stench in the shit-shack is penetrating but it's just that: a stench that can be washed off. The stench in the confessional is there forever and can't be gotten rid of. It's the kind of stink that originates in corrupt souls and that can never be washed away. If one confesses his sins in the shit-shack only God hears you. If you confess in the confessional at Thebes House, the whole orphanage hears you. It's a lair of wolves leading the meek to their spiritual corruption. Jim can still feel the burning pain of the bamboo cane. The son of a bitch put all his strength in whipping the crap out of the boy — literally whipping the crap out. The tears stream down Jim's eyes like a spring. His hate and anger for the orphanage, for the Wobbs, for the priests, for the bishop, whirls in him like a demon gone mad. He stands up and

---

[23] small, little

fetches the shit-bucket from under the stool. He got used to the stench by now. It's just shit. What he never got used to is the putrid reek of the hypocrites of Thebes House. The shit-shack, although small, cold, and smelly, is far safer and pleasant than the portico of hell called Thebes House.

"Did ye wash yer hands?" asks Shaw. Jim is back from doing the can.

"Yes, Mr. Shaw."

"Took ye longer than usual to do the can," utters the old man sharply.

"The stench was persistent Mr. Shaw."

"Och! The beans! Aye, that's the fall-out of beans, ma lad. They're gaud far ye, but the keech[24] reeks worse than festered boak[25]!" snickers Shaw.

"Sit down, let's have supper! No beans tonight," assures the old man.

After supper the old man pulls out the chess set.

"It's been a week, lad, we haven't played." He pours the pieces on the board and picks one white pawn and one black pawn: one in each hand. Shaw shuffles the pawns behind his back and nods to Jim.

"Left," utters Jim.

"Ma left or yer left?" replies Shaw. Jim points a finger to Shaw's left.

"Black! Poor ye laddie!" chuckles Shaw. The game starts; after ten or so moves Shaw's face gets serious. He looks up at Jim puzzled. The young fellow cracks a crooked smile. Shaw sits straight up and focuses his thoughts on the chess game. It is eerily quiet, no wind, no rain, no thumping swells. Hesitantly Shaw makes his move. The boy makes a counter move immediately after.

---

[24] excrement, shit
[25] vomit, puke

The old man stands up and walks up and down looking at the board in deep thought. Jim leans back and the smirk on his face doesn't vanish. Shaw sits down and is visibly nervous. The light flash from the tower is clearly visible through the kitchen window. It's a clear and snell[26] winter night. The old man lights his pipe.

"Well, Mr. Shaw? What's going to be?" asks Jim in a stinging tone of voice. The young man has, up to date, not won a single chess game from the old man. However, tonight something has changed. Shaw makes his move. Jim follows up immediately.

"Check!" yelps Jim. The lighthouse keeper puts his pipe aside and leans closer to the board.

"You're going to be checkmate in three moves," gloats Jim demonstratively. The old man ponders his next move and cautiously moves the rook. Jim follows with a short hop of his queen.

"You're dead Mr. Shaw, two more moves." Shaw looks at the lad with a penetrating gaze. The old man moves the rook again. Jim follows with a knight. Shaw's eyes grow big, grabs his pipe, and starts fidgeting with it. The lighthouse keeper sees what's coming and topples his king over as a sign of defeat. He slowly leans back somewhat in disbelieve. Jim grins and gloats; this is his first victory against Lewis Shaw, the chess man! The young man stands up, goes in his room, and comes back with a book in his hand. He demonstratively puts it in front of Shaw.

"That's ma chess book," gripes the old man.

"That's the book you took from that shelf many weeks ago and told me I wasn't ready for it, remember?" Shaw doesn't budge.

"Am I ready now, Mr. Shaw?" The lighthouse keeper stands up, grabs the book, the box and chess board, and disappears in his room. Jim leans back and smiles.

---

[26] bitter or very cold weather

IX

The foghorn blurts that annoying low-pitched reverberation; it wails like a sick cow. A dense fog covers Hell's Mouth. There is no wind and the morning is cold. Although it is daytime, the light is on but barely visible. The days pass by and winter seems to have laid anchor at the Skerries and doesn't want to leave. Maggy the cow doesn't seem bothered by the horn. She passively stands there while Jim milks her. The boy's daily duties are still mostly house chores. However, the old man taught him how to operate the foghorn. Now the blurting bawling beast falls under Jim's responsibility to turn on when fog rolls in. Jim cracks a smile. He remembers the old man's stupefied face that night, a couple of weeks ago, when he beat the old man at his own game, chess. Since that night they have not played, and Shaw has the chess book kidnapped in his quarters: the only room of the compound that Jim may not enter. *'He is brooding something'* thinks Jim. The man is yearning for chess revenge.

"He's probably plotting his comeback, isn't he Maggy?" chuckles Jim. The door opens and Shaw enters the barn.

"Is he milking ye gaud, Maggy?" The cow just gazes at Shaw. The man limps to the back end of the barn and rummages for something.

"Och, here it is!" Shaw pulls a case from a shelf and leaves the barn. Jim is about done milking the cow and ushers Maggy back to her stall. The sheep, pigs, and chicken run around in the barn trying to dodge Jim. He leaves the barn, milk bucket in hand, and heads to the main cottage. The fog is still quite dense. The foghorn blurts its awful sound incessantly. The boy puts the milk bucket on the kitchen counter.

"Stay here lad. This is something ye must know." Shaw retrieves a weird looking contraption from the cabinet underneath the kitchen counter. The thing looks like two copper tubing coils. One of the coils he submerges in boiling water and the other coil in a large bowl of fresh cold water. The old man connects the coils with black rubber tubing and hooks the front-end coil to a small hand pump. The exit pipe of the back-end coil is placed in a porcelain jar.

"Now lad, pay attention. Lesson one: never drink milk straight from the cow. It can make ye sick or kill ye. Second: make sure the coils and rubber tubing are washed and well cleaned. Wash the inside of the coils with vinegar and rinse them well with boiled water afterwards. Third: the same for the hand pump and the porcelain retriever. Ye follow?" Jim nods.

"Gaud, now, place the fresh milk bucket here." Jim puts the large milk bucket next to the hand pump.

"Och, forgot to tell ye, always wash yer hands after milking and before doing this procedure." The boy washes his hands thoroughly. Shaw slides the suction pipe of the hand pump in the milk bucket and slowly cranks the pump lever up and down. The milk passes first through the hot coil and subsequently through the cold coil before ending up in the porcelain jar. The old man pumps the milk with a steady slow rhythm. After all of the milk is pumped through, he removes the hand pump, and instructs Jim to rinse the bucket with boiled water. Once the bucket is rinsed, Shaw pours the milk contained in the porcelain jar back into the bucket and repeats the same procedure again. He passes the milk three times through the coils. After the last pass Shaw seals the porcelain jar and stores it in the cool provision room. The old man washes his hands, grabs his smoking pipe, and fills it with tobacco.

"That procedure you just saw is essential, ma lad. It prevents dangerous bugs to grow in the milk. Ye can't boil the milk like we dae with water; it clogs. Ye have to heat it slowly. Dinnae ever drink unprocessed milk," stresses Shaw unwaveringly. Jim washes the coils and bucket and stores them under the kitchen counter. While the boy washes the coils, Shaw steps into his room and fetches a book. He puts it on the table and motions Jim to take it.

"Ye've learned yer chess game from the book. Now, show me ye can learn how to handle the lighthouse driving engine from the manual," mocks Shaw. Jim picks up the manual and opens it.

"I've never worked on engines before, Mr. Shaw," utters Jim in a low voice.

"Ye've never played chess before," scoffs the old man.

"True, but chess and engines are different things," replies the young man.

"Neay, they are not. Follow the instructions and ye'll dae alright."

"What do you want me to do with the engine?" asks Jim cautiously.

"Study it!" responds Shaw immediately.

"When the time is right, we'll take it apart and reassemble it. Ye have till summer to study it. In summertime, when the days are langer, we'll work on the engine; be ready!" Shaw stands up, cleans the smoking pipe, and leaves the cottage to do work in the lighthouse. Jim browses through the manual. He looks at the drawings and at the strange names of the engine parts. *'I can't learn this from a book'*, he thinks anxiously, *'I don't know anything about this!'*

The days pass by. The miserable grey winter weather hangs on unremitting. The rain, the fog, the cold, and snow exhaust one's spirit; not to mention the dread of the never ending daily mundane chores that numb one's mind into a sleep like state. Besides all of this, Jim struggles to figure out the terms and strange technical names in the engine manual. When he asks Shaw to clarify a technical term, the old man just shrugs and says "ye'll figure it out." Jim gets no help at all from the old geezer. One clear but cold night, after doing the can, Jim steps into the main cottage room and slams the manual on the table. Standing at the kitchen counter, Shaw indifferently looks at Jim and keeps doing the cooking.

"I don't get this damn thing!" blurts Jim. The old man doesn't budge.

"Is this your revenge for getting mashed at chess? You know I haven't a clue what all this engine stuff is! You know that without help I won't understand a knack of what's in the manual. You're enjoying this, aren't you?" The old man puts the stirrer down, grabs his pipe, lights it, and sits down at the table looking at Jim with a rude stare.

"Did ye wash yer hands?" asks Shaw sarcastically. Jim demonstratively shows him his hands without saying a word.

"Gaud! Ah wouldn't like ye to soil ma book with dirty hands."

"You can keep your damn book!" retorts Jim immediately.

"Och? Ye're cussing[27] now. Didnae[28] learn that from me!"

"Didn't learn squat from you except mundane chores," fumes Jim.

"Perhaps! But surely not cussing. Blaspheming dinnae make you a man; only eejits[29] cuss," utters the old man calmly.

"Are ye an eejit lad?" Jim knows what "eejit" means. He's heard plenty of that word in Thebes House. That's what Sister

---

[27] cursing
[28] didn't
[29] idiots

Constanza called Jim, eejit! What a fiend of a woman she is. Jim was no star at learning Latin. Sister Constanza is the classical languages teacher at Thebes House, Latin and Greek. Jim hates both languages. The boy's memory fleets back to the spring of 1948. In Latin class Sister Constanza asks Jim to name an animal in Latin. Jim stands up and blurts "Porcus."[30].

"Gaud!" praises Sister Constanza, "And what is porcus in Greek?" Immediately Jim hollers "Constanza!" The other pupil's eyes turn large like saucers. The nun turns fiery red, steps down from the teacher's platform, walks over to Jim and unrestrainedly punches the boy flat on the nose. The blood gushes out all over his desk. Following the punch comes a skelp from Sister Constanza further splattering the spurting blood all over the place.

"Go to yer room, eejit!" shrieks the nun. The boy picks up his bloodied stuff and calmly makes his way out of the classroom.

"Wobb!" whispers Jim. That same night Jim got locked up in the catacombs; the same dreadful room he got caned by Father Murray a couple of years ago. Murray's caning in 1946 was not the last time Jim got a taste of the bamboo wicker. This time he got it from Father Duncan; the same priest he confessed his witnessing of the lewd acts of Father Murray and Sister Mary on Christmas Eve 1946. Ten lashes and a broken nose; it could be worse thought Jim. He's seen worse at Thebes House. He's seen blood. He's seen suffering. He's seen death. All kept a 'holy' secret.

---

[30] pig

X

April 12th, 1951. Spring finally arrives. The night was foggy and the blurting monster on the south tower made its horrible sound the whole night. However, the morning is clear, the fog lifted, and Jim shuts the foghorn off. *'What a relief'* murmurs Jim in his mind. Red and white poppies cover the desolate plateau of Muckle Skerry. Jim savors the colorful vista while standing on top of the south tower. The morning is cold but fresh and invigorating. The eastern sun washes the island with a reddish glow that blends with the vibrant hues of the small flowers. The breeze is calm and pleasant. In the courtyard he sees Shaw opening the barn door and ushering the animals to get out of the barn. Maggy rushes out of the barn into the courtyard followed by the sheep, chickens, and the pigs. They are visibly happy. After months of being locked up in the barn finally they get to roam around the open field. Maggy and the sheep run into the wide-open corral south of the tower complex and immediately start tasting the fresh grass. What a sight it is. Maggy runs around and makes funny jumps of joy. The sheep dedicate themselves immediately to grazing; they munch flowers and all. What a difference with the gloomy grey days of winter. *He maketh me lie down in green pastures: "He leadeth me beside the still waters"*. That is part of one of Mr. Shaw's favorite prayers at supper. *'Is it this what he means with that'* wonders the boy. The green and colorful plateau of Muckle Skerry on this sun washed spring morning sure makes one feel that way. A warm feeling of exultation fills Jim's heart; a feeling he has never felt at Thebes House.

A faint horn blow disturbs Jim's daydream. He peers southward in the direction from where the horn sound is coming. The weather is clear, and he spots a boat heading towards Muckle Skerry.

"Jim! Get doon[31]! The Guards are coming!" hollers Shaw from the courtyard. The boy rushes down the spiral staircase and meets Shaw in the yard.

"The Guards Mr. Shaw?" inquires Jim confused.

"Aye, they bring fuel to Muckle every spring and autumn. Come, come, we need to lower *Cheers*[32]!" The two men rush to the cove where Cheers hangs on the crane. Shaw limps down the concrete stairs to the cove while Jim winches down the sloop. The Guard's vessel is not a boat. It's much bigger than that. Slowly the big vessel maneuvers close to where Hope is moored and lay down anchor. The name of the vessel is *H.M.C.G. Sparrow* and on deck are some officers dressed in white uniforms. They wave and Shaw waves back. The sea is calm, and the rowing goes smooth. On the port side of the ship a crew of sailors lower a much bigger sloop than Cheers loaded with what looks like large metal cans similar to the ones stored in the lighthouse tower.

"Hullo there Shaw!" hollers an officer from the ship's deck.

"Ahoy!" blurts Shaw. The old man maneuvers Cheers to get close behind the bigger sloop. The sailors throw a rope to fasten Cheers to the bigger boat. A rope ladder is lowered, and two officers climb down to the big sloop. From the side of the ship, sailors lower big sacks of coal to be loaded on Cheers. Jim is fascinated by the majestic Coast Guard ship. The Coast Guard sloop, loaded with fuel cans, tows Cheers into the cove. Once inside the cove, the sailors unload the fuel cans and the coal from the boats. The officer shakes hands with Shaw.

---

[31] down
[32] *Cheers* is the name of the sloop

"How have you been, Shaw?" asks the officer cheerfully.

"Gaud! Can't complain," replies Shaw. "How are ye doing Lieutenant Blake?"

"Very well thank you. I see you've got help," states the officer while pointing at Jim.

"Aye! A Sassenach like ye. Good lad. Crabbit[33] sometimes, but braw[34] young lad. A cup of coffee Lieutenant?"

"Certainly!" replies the officer happily. He utters some orders to the men, and they proceed to haul up the fuel cans and carry them to the lighthouse storeroom. On their way to the main cottage, the Lieutenant lights a cigarette and asks Jim, "since when do you work here?"

"November last year, sir," answers the young man. Shaw limps his way quickly to the cottage to put coffee. Jim and the officer take their time.

"What do you think of the old man?" inquires Lt. Blake.

"How so?" asks Jim a little confused.

"Well, you are the third apprentice of Shaw in six years. The two before you didn't go well." Jim stops.

"Didn't go well?" asks Jim anxiously, "what do you mean?" The Lieutenant smiles, takes a drag, and explains: "The first one drowned and the second couldn't handle the old man, I guess."

"Drowned?" utters Jim in a shaky voice.

"Yup! His body was found a day later in that same cove we unload the provisions. I brought the body back to the mainland."

"And the second one?" asks Jim.

"Brought him back to Groats; he would not stay another night here. He kept saying that it spooks." Jim gets the creeps. Shaw never told him about this. Spooks? Ghosts? Demons?

---

[33] ill-tempered
[34] fine

The main room is warm and pleasant. Shaw serves the coffee and sits down at the round table. The officer takes off his cap, puts it on the table, and takes a sip.

"Good coffee, Shaw! Haven't lost the touch, I see."

"The trick is in the roasting," answers Shaw.

"How is Old Reid? Did he tickle the boy yet?" chuckles the Lieutenant.

"Och, havers[35] auld lad! Ye know that's all havers!" rebukes Shaw immediately.

"That's not what the previous chap said. He was scared out of his socks when I ferried him back to Groats."

"Och, that Jessie[36]! He was scared of his own shadow."

"Who is Old Reid?" asks Jim anxiously.

"All glaikit[37] stories ma lad. Only gowks[38] believe that kind of havers!" murmurs Shaw.

The Lieutenant leans forward, takes a drag, and tells the story:

"Old Reid was one of Muckle Skerry's principal lighthouse keepers in the mid nineteen century. He and his family lived here in this cottage. It is said that a strange disease killed his wife and sons and that Old Reid lost his mind while alone on Muckle. Some say he killed himself. Others assure that he sold his soul to the devil and the devil himself took his soul. Anyways, his body was never found. Old Reid just vanished from the face of the earth. Folk stories, my boy, just that." The hair on Jim's neck stand straight up. Shaw pours the officer a second cup of coffee.

---

[35] nonsense
[36] coward
[37] stupid
[38] fools

"Ye're scaring the lad, Lieutenant. Auld Reid is lang gone; may his soul rest in peace. Now, enough of the balahoochie stories. Tell me, what's new with our lads in Korea?"

"Rough, old man. The Chinese and North Koreans give tough resistance. The fighting is fierce," informs the officer in a somewhat concerned tone of voice.

"They dinnae learn, dae they?" murmurs Shaw. "Four bloody wars in ma lifetime. Ah can barely believe it maself."

"Well, Shaw, time to move on! Thank God for spring; it was a long winter this one. Oh, I know you're going to protest Shaw, but I brought you the radio again. We think you should be in communication with us."

"Neay! Told ye already, dinnae need a radio. Been here for thirty years without radio; Ah'm still here, ain't Ah?" bawls the old man. The Lieutenant looks at Jim "will you take it please?" Jim looks at Shaw. The old man throws his hands in the air and says, "ye handle it, lad, Ah dinnae ken how to work that thing." Lt. Blake smiles, puts on his cap, and quickly steps to the front door.

"Clarke bring the radio!" hollers the officer to a sailor outside. In a nick of time the sailor brings two cases and puts them in the room. The Lieutenant opens the large case. In it is a brand-new contraption with dials and knobs.

"Here is the manual, chap, read it, easy stuff." He then opens the smaller case and pulls out a device with a crank handle on it. He connects two wires to the radio and cranks the handle. The thing makes a rickety cracking sound.

"Pay attention chap; this is to load up the radio batteries. You tie up the red wire to the red knob and the black one to the black knob then you crank the lever for twenty minutes every day. It keeps the battery loaded. Do you understand? Here try it." Blake hands the crank box over to the boy. Jim gives the thing a few cranks.

"Easy, isn't it? Anyone can do it," claims the officer. He shakes hands with Shaw and steps outside. Jim follows him to the cove.

"Excuse me sir," utters Jim in a low voice.

"Why do the town people call Mr. Shaw Crazy Lew? Do you know?" The Lieutenant lights a cigarette and smiles.

"They say he's possessed by Old Reid," chuckles the officer. Jim freezes up.

"Oh, you know, chap, town folk's stories. It's all baloney, don't worry about it. Old Shaw may be a lot of things but crazy or possessed he's not." The officer and Jim shake hands and he makes his way down to the cove. 'Cheers' is already hanging on the crane. The sailors took care of everything. The officer steps into the Coast Guard sloop and hollers to Jim, "say hullo to Old Reid for me, will you? Take care fellow! Keep in touch through the radio. See you in autumn." Jim hesitantly waves back. They make their way back on board the ship, haul up the sloop, and sail away. H.M.C.G Sparrow utters two short bursts of the horn as goodbye. Jim waves them farewell.

Back in the cottage, Jim unpacks the radio. He's like a kid with a new toy.

"May I keep it in my room?" he asks Shaw. The old man just shrugs and smokes the pipe. The young man picks up the two cases and goes to his room.

"Ye got chores to dae!" hollers Shaw.

"Yes Mr. Shaw, I'll be out in just a minute." A faint smile appears on the old man's face. He saw something in Jim today he was anxious to see for months; he saw a spark of life in the boy.

After supper, Shaw demonstratively drops the chess board on the table. The sudden noise makes Jim jump in his chair. The old man opens the box, pours the pieces on the board, and with a smile picks a white and a black pawn.

"Ye get white. No need to choose tonight. Ah'll play black and Ah'll give yer wee bahookie[39] a fine chess skelping tonight." The pieces are set, and the game begins. This is the first game they play since the night Jim won. Shaw's eyes glisten in the lamp light; he's thirsting for revenge. All that time the old man kept the chess book and pieces well hidden in his quarters. Jim opens with the traditional king's pawn. Shaw follows with the queen's pawn: a different move he never played before. The boy looks at the old man and smiles. Shaw smiles back. After about six moves, Jim utters, "you have done your studies Mr. Shaw."

"Ah hope ye remember yers," replies the old man sarcastically. The game turns into a real psychological battle. Shaw smokes the pipe and blows the smoke purposely in Jim's face.

"Would you stop that!" murmurs the boy annoyed.

"Bothers ye?" asks Shaw.

"Yes!" retorts Jim.

"So sorry," utters the old man but he doesn't stop smoking Jim up. Jim stands up and fetches the radio crank charger from his room. He sits down at the table and starts cranking the device. The rickety-clicking sound it makes drives the geebees on Shaw's nerves.

"Put that away!" grumbles the old man.

"Put off the pipe," rebukes Jim. Shaw's eyes pierce Jim fiercely. The young man doesn't flinch. Slowly the old man empties the pipe in the clay ashtray. Jim puts the crank charger on the table. The game continues. It is evident that the principal lighthouse keeper beefed up his chess game, but the boy is giving him a hell of a fight. At the fifteenth move Shaw goes into attack.

---

[39] buttocks

He expressively slides a rook into a key offensive position. He stands up, claps his hand, and chuckles like a kid in a candy store.

"May I smoke over there, laddie?" asks Shaw in a mocking tone.

"If I may crank the charger over there," answers Jim sardonically.

"Ha! Ha! Let's see what ye dae now, frein[40]!" smirks the old man. Jim tries to concentrate but the old man starts to rummage in the kitchen making a lot of noise moving pans and plates around.

"Can't you just sit down and play Mr. Shaw?" bawls Jim.

"Hold on laddie, Ah'm looking for the pudding bowls. Ye want some pudding?"

"No!" retorts Jim loudly.

"Too bad lad, it's delicious." The boy makes his move: a defensive one. Shaw returns to his seat with a bowl of pudding in hand. His eyes scan the chess board as if possessed. Suddenly, Shaw puts a hand on his nose, "Mighty me! Did ye fairt[41]?" Jim smiles, "the colcannon Mr. Shaw. Uncontrollable!" Shaw stands up and opens the kitchen window. A cold breeze rushes in the room.

"Keep yer erse[42] shut!" hollers Shaw and sits back down. Shaw dives into the game. Jim blows wind again.

"Hoots! Are ye gaunnae stop that!" hollers Shaw furiously.

"Sorry," mutters Jim. Shaw puts his head in his hand and scans the board intensely. He picks up his queen and slams it across the board.

"Now! Take that laddie! See what ye dae now." Jim leans closer to the board. The old man is serious. Suddenly a flabby blubber sound is heard followed by a wicked stench.

---

[40] friend
[41] fart
[42] arse

"Sorry lad, ate the same colcannon ye did," grins Shaw. He leans back and starts whistling a Scottish tune. Jim looks up, "would you please stop!" Shaw grins, "why dinnae ye like it?" Jim focuses back on the chess board. Shaw leans back, smiling, and makes an annoying squeaky sound with the chair. Jim stands up, grabs his coat, and goes outside.

"Ye quit lad?" hollers Shaw.

"No, I'll be right back!" yells the boy. A few minutes later the foghorn starts bawling its loud awful sound. Jim returns to the cottage.

"Why ye start the horn? There is no fog?" utters Shaw.

"There's going to be fog soon," replies Jim.

"How dae ye ken that?" Jim sits down and resumes the game. He makes a simple move with a pawn. Every so many seconds the hollering beast outside makes its deeply annoying low pitch noise. As Shaw reaches out for his knight, the foghorn blurts its hellish blare.

"Hear that Mr. Shaw? The horn tells you it's a bad move." Shaw looks with a piercing gaze at Jim. He reaches out for the knight and the foghorn repeats its blurt again.

"Listen to the horn Mr. Shaw." The old man briskly stands up tipping his chair over. He puts on his impermeable and steps outside. A couple of minutes later the foghorn goes mute. He comes back in, takes his coat off, picks up the chair and sits down.

"There's no fog tonight. Leave the thing off," grumbles Shaw and concentrates on the game. He moves the knight.

"Should have heeded the horn Mr. Shaw, here you go." Jim moves his queen a few squares to the front. Shaw follows immediately with a rook. Jim returns the queen to safety. Shaw stands up and briskly moves the knight.

"Check, ye wee bum!" Jim leans forward. He did not see that move. The old man is getting dangerously close. Jim concentrates on what to do. The man got him on the run.

"Ha! Genius, what dae ye dae now?" Jim moves his king to the left. Shaw immediately spears his queen forward.

"Gaunnae get ye laddie," chuckles Shaw.

"Are you sure about that," utters Jim sharply and in a sweeping move takes Shaw's queen with a bishop. The old man's eyes grow big and he drops the pipe on the floor.

"Neay! Neay! Where did that come from?" stutters the old man in disbelief. Jim leans back and smiles.

"Saving it for your queen, Mr. Shaw," gloats the young man. Shaw slowly leans back.

"You're too hasty, Mr. Shaw." Jim rubs it in. The old man sits there flabbergasted for a minute. He pulls himself together and retracts the rook back to his line of defense.

The chess battle rages on. Jim, having the upper hand, goes into attack. Shaw puts a fierce defense. In his haste Jim makes a mistake and Shaw captures Jim's queen.

"The devil knows more by being auld then by being the devil," murmurs Shaw grinning. The game is about even. Shaw tries to attack the boy on his left flank. Jim pulverizes the attack and immediately pushes on Shaw's left flank. The sea-saw of attack and defense goes on for hours. None of the two men thinks of giving up. At about eleven o'clock the game finally ends in a stalemate. Shaw stretches out his hand and Jim shakes it.

"Ye're a wee lucky bastart but ye got grit. I like that," utters the old man in a raspy voice. He stands up, fetches the chess book from his room, and gives it to Jim.

"It's yers now. The chess game too. Ye'll make a hell of a better chess player than Ah. Use it well." The old man silently retreats to his room. Jim just sits there quiet. From Shaw's quarters a soft sound fills the cottage: the sound of a bagpipe playing the song Auld Lang Syne. Jim listens to it as if riveted to the chair. The sound is so mellow and perfect. It's the first time Jim hears it. He didn't know Shaw played the pipes. The song ends and the room goes quiet. The sliver of light under Shaw's door goes dark. Jim stands up, closes the kitchen window, blows out the lamps and goes to bed. It was an interesting day.

XI

It's the end of May and springtime is in all its glory. Now and then it drizzles and gets foggy, but overall, the weather behaves fantastically. Muckle Skerry in spring is way different than Muckle Skerry in winter. Maggy and the sheep graze in the outer yard and the pigs do their thing in a fenced mud pool at the edge of the inner courtyard. The chickens, well, they do their chicken thing. The morning is bright and shiny. Jim is cleaning the barn when he hears a whistle outside. It's Shaw standing in the courtyard dressed in a leather apron and a wooden case in hand. "Come here lad! Got to teach ye something," hollers the old man. Jim leans the hay fork on the door and approaches Shaw.

"Here haud this." Shaw hands the boy a coiled rope, puts down the wooden case, and opens it. In the case there is a set of knives of all shapes: crooked, small, and large. Shaw pulls out a leather strap from the case and a long-crooked knife. He sharpens the knife by rasping it on the strap.

"What's this for?" asks Jim somewhat anxious.

"We're gaunnae make haggis, ma lad," answers Shaw with a smile.

"Haggis? What's that?" inquires Jim.

"Didnae the nuns make Haggis in Aberdeen lad? Ten years in Scotland and ye haven't eaten haggis? What kind o' nuns are these?" chuckles the old man.

"Here haud this. Be careful, it's sharp. Hand me the rope." Jim hands him the rope and Shaw steps to the outer yard. He slowly approaches one of the sheep and ties the rope around its neck. The poor thing bleats loud in agony. Shaw wrestles the animal and manages to tie its legs together. The horrid bleating fills Jim's heart with anguish and compassion for the poor animal. Shaw drags the sheep to the yard wall and motions Jim to come with the knife. The awful sound of the poor beast grows louder. It is an awful and desperate loud shriek. The poor thing wiggles and struggles to try to escape but Shaw's rope knots won't budge.

"Come here lad, hurry! Don't be afraid. It'll be over in a wink." Hesitantly Jim approaches the awful scene. The loud squeals and shrieks of the poor beast give Jim the shivers.

"I'll hold it and pull its heid up. Use the hook knife to slit its throat in one smooth motion, ye follow?" Jim is in horror. He'd never done something like this: killing. He drops the knife. The animal gets more anxious and the cries are deafening. Shaw grabs the animal by the chin and lifts its head up. Jim just stands there frozen.

"What are ye doing? Pick up the hook! Slit the throat, quick! Right here!" hollers Shaw. Jim doesn't budge.

"Jim! Pick up the knife! Come lad ye can do it!" bawls the old man while wrestling the animal. The animal jerks violently with its legs and the horrible squeals get louder and more heart wrenching. Jim is paralyzed. He can't do it.

"Ye Jessie! Get me the knife!" yells Shaw furiously. Jim slowly picks up the knife and hands it over to Shaw who in a swift move slits the animal's throat. The blood squirts out all over the two men. The poor thing's legs jerk a few more times and then it is quiet. Shaw's face, hands, and apron are all bloodied. Jim looks at his vest and sees a long streak of blood on it. Shaw hands over the bloody knife to Jim and drags the dead sheep to a large wooden table in the courtyard. The boy stands alone knife in hand.

"Hey! We ain't got all day, ye know!" hollers Shaw. Jim jumps out of his paralysis and walks over to the old man.

"Gimme that. Now wash yer hands," orders Shaw. The old man lifts the dead animal and lays it down on the table. He washes his face and hands and places the case with the knives on top of the table. Shaw grabs Jim by the arm and yanks him closer.

"Get yerself together, will ye! Pay attention, Ah'm gaunnae gut and clean the animal. Pay gaud attention 'cause the next one ye kill, gut, and clean!" Jim doesn't budge.

"Ah'm gaunnae show ye how to gut the sheep to make haggis. Pass me that thin knife." Jim passes him the knife. Skillfully Shaw guts the animal, and nothing goes to waste. The boy stands there in horror. The awful smell of the intestines gives him nausea. After an hour and a half, Shaw finishes the gruesome job. Everything is saved: stomach, liver, lungs, all of it. Shaw takes off the apron, washes it, and puts it to dry. All around are bloody bowls full of flesh, gut, bones, and more. He washes his face and hands again and gathers the set of knives. The old man washes the knives carefully, dries them up, and places them in the case.

"Bring them bowls to the storeroom, will ye!" orders Shaw sternly and walks away to the main cottage. *'My God'* thinks Jim, *'the poor animal was so happy this morning. Look at it now!'* He picks up the first bowl and hauls it to the storeroom. Slowly he brings the rest of the bowls to the larder. His mind is blank and his stomach upside down. The horrible squeal of the animal reverberates in his head. He can't get it out. The eyes, the eyes of the poor thing were bewildered, desperate, anxious. The wide eyes told Jim all that was going through the animal's mind; it knew death was near.

"The Lord is ma Light and salvation — whom shall Ah fear? The Lord is the stronghold of ma life — of whom shall Ah be afraid? One thing Ah ask from the Lord, this only Ah seek: that Ah may dwell in the house of the Lord all the days of ma life, to gaze on the beauty of the Lord and to seek him in his temple. Thank ye Lord for our meal tonight. Amen."

Jim remains quiet. The night is chilly, and the fog rolled in. The beast on the south tower blurts its horrible sound. The growl of the foghorn mixes with the high pitch squeal in Jim's head. He just sits there and stares at the food.

"Ye're not eating," mumbles Shaw. The boy remains quiet.

"It's the killing, ain't it lad?" Jim fixes his gaze on Shaw. The old man moves his plate away and leans back.

"The squealing, the jerking, the blood, aye, horrid business, but necessary." The old man stands up and fetches his pipe from the shelf.

"Ye see lad, nothing goes to waste. All of the animal is consumed and that is the way it should be. Tomorrow we have haggis for dinner. Ye'll like it. Pickled all this afternoon. What ye saw today is part o' life ma frein. The creature gave its life for us to have food on the table. That's why we must consume all of it in respect for the deid[43] animal. The killing must be quick to lessen the suffering. The more ye hesitate, the worse it is for the poor thing."

"I'm sorry Mr. Shaw, but I couldn't do it. It's the horrible squeal and the eyes," utters Jim almost whispering. Shaw sits down and lights the pipe.

---

[43] dead

"Aye. The eyes, the squeals, aye lad, it bounces around in yer heid; it never leaves." Jim pushes his plate away and leans forward. The tears well up in his eyes.

"I'm not hungry tonight, Mr. Shaw," utters the young man softly. Shaw nods slowly.

"Ye must understand one thing lad, killing the sheep ain't murder. There is no shame to it as long as we respect the offering and sacrifice made."

Jim lowers his head and murmurs, "why all the suffering? Why if God is so good and merciful some must die for others to live? Why didn't God just make things in such a way that all can eat without killing, without suffering?" Shaw takes a deep drag on the pipe.

"Ah dinnae ken lad, who are we to question the ways of the Lord? He made it once so in Paradise, but we screwed up!" Jim briskly stands up.

"Do you really believe that nonsense?" retorts the boy. "All fabricated rubbish!"

"Och, what dae ye believe?" inquires Shaw sharply. Jim turns and leans on the table and faces Shaw with raging fiery eyes.

"I believe all this god stuff, this, this, crucifix and Jesus thing, this saints and martyr baloney is made up to keep the meek stupid and the savvy in power! It's all a scam, a hoax! There is no heaven. There is no hell. There's just this: earth, suffering, and dying. God is dead and men killed him."

"Ye can't go in life like that lad. Ye have a rage that is festering in ye. The ire will eventually kill ye. Ah dinnae ken why ye're so wrathful. Ye'll be lang deid[44], ye know?" The old man puts the pipe aside and looks at Jim with piercing eyes.

---

[44] "Ye'll be lang deid" – Scottish saying meaning enjoy life because you'll be a long time dead

"Why are ye so ireful, lad? It's deep under yer skin." Without saying a word, Jim retires to his room. Shaw grabs a book from the shelf, sits down, brings the lamp closer, and browses through the pages. In between the belches of the foghorn, Shaw hears the rickety-clicking sound of the battery charger and smiles.

XII

It's a drizzly June Monday. It's not cold but the sky is grey, and the drizzle is incessant. Shaw boarded Hope early in the morning and sailed to John o' Groats to do the messages. Jim gave him a letter he wrote yesterday to post to Aberdeen; it's the first letter to his former orphan roommates at Thebes House. He addressed it to Herbert, his best friend.

Muckle Skerry, Sunday, June 10th, 1951
Dear Herbert,
My apologies for not writing sooner. I've been assigned a job as apprentice lighthouse keeper on Muckle Skerry. Look it up on the map; it's a tiny island north-east of the northern tip of mainland Scotland. I work for Mr. Shaw and it's only the two of us here on the island. Mr. Shaw must be in his 70's but is a big man and very energetic. I must say that it's quite a bore here. The weather is mostly foul, and the daily chores are truly mind numbing. Mr. Shaw thought me how to operate the foghorn; a big machine that makes the most horrible noise you can imagine. It sounds like a loud and long belch. I've also got a radio. It was given to me by a Coast Guard officer. It works great. You should have seen the Coast Guard ship. What a fantastic thing it is. Soon Mr. Shaw will be teaching me how to operate the lighthouse. To be honest, I don't

really want to stay here. I want to travel to India and Australia. Remember how we used to play adventurers and imagine we're traveling the world? Someday I hope that will come true, but for now it's Muckle Skerry. Please give my regards to Orville and Norman and if you like, read this letter to them. I miss you my friends, but I don't miss Thebes House. I'll try to write more often.
    All the best, sincerely, Jim.

    Jim's first chore every Monday is to clean the roof gutters that collect rainwater to the water cistern. While putting on his coat Jim notices that the door to Shaw's quarters is cracked open. He grabs the door handle and closes it. A strange feeling of curiosity gets a hold of the young man. Shaw's room is off limits, but Jim wonders why. He cracks open the door and peeks inside. The bed is meticulously made up: square and precise. The room is much bigger than Jim's. Slowly he steps inside the room. Next to the bed is a small night table with a framed picture on it. It's the portrait of a young woman holding a rose. She has a beautiful face and a mysterious smile. Hanging on the wall above the bedhead is a large painting of the Muckle Skerry lighthouse. The signature on the canvas says 'Banach 1898'. That must be Banach's, the former principal lighthouse keeper and Shaw's teacher.

    Next to the bed, on the west wall of the room is a large, wall-to-wall, book case. Jim gets closer to it. *Plato – The Dialogues, Treasure Island, Aristotle, Hume, An introduction to Geometry, Crime and Punishment, Meditations by Marcus Aurelius,* and on and on, there are hundreds of books in the book case all unknown to Jim. On the south wall of the room there is a large wardrobe and a big trunk next to it. Jim opens the trunk and his eyes grow big. The trunk is stuffed with military uniforms, belts, kilts, bonnets with red feathers, a helmet, and a revolver. Jim carefully fetches the handgun and holds it in awe. It has the word *Enfield* etched on it.

Courtesy of the Muckle Skerry Archives at The John o' Groats Foundation.

    He puts it back and fetches a wooden box. In it are a bunch of medals. One of the medals has a red and blue ribbon with a bar on it and on one side of the medal is the image of King George the fifth and on the other side the words 'For Distinguished Conduct on the Field' are etched. Another medal looks like a star with two crossed swords on it. It has a red, white, and blue ribbon with a metal bar sown to it saying '5th AUG. – 22nd NOV. 1914'. On the backside of the star medal is etched 'D-332 SGT. L. Shaw. 3

SCOTS'. Carefully Jim closes the medal box and puts it back in the trunk. *'The man was in the army'* contemplates Jim, *'that's the Black Watch the wheelchair man in Groats was talking about. Shaw must be a war hero to have all those medals!'* Slowly Jim opens the wardrobe. Hanging in it are merely regular clothes, but in the back-corner Jim sees something that makes his heart pounce: a rifle. The boy carefully retrieves the weapon from the closet. It is heavy and has the same etched word on it: *Enfield*. Jim looks at it in awe. It looks well maintained: all glossy and shiny. Slowly the boy puts the rifle on his shoulder and stands in attention. With his left hand he makes a salute and smiles. *'Maybe Mr. Shaw will let me practice with it'*, he fancies. He puts the rifle back in the wardrobe, closes it, and leaves the room. He runs out of the cottage, fetches his gutter cleaning gear, and starts his chore. Jim is all smiles.

Shaw returns from Groats in the afternoon and Jim helps store the new provisions. The old man goes into the cottage, washes his hands, and starts preparing supper. The last chore of the day, as always, is the can. However, today Jim didn't mind doing the can. The day is all drizzles, but Jim's spirit is high. The uniforms, the medals, the guns, all whirl around the whole day in Jim's mind. Shaw never talks about the military. Except for the chess book, he never lends Jim a book from his private collection. *'Why?'* wonders Jim. *'I can read'* ponders the young man. *'He'll probably say that I'm not ready yet just like the chess book.'* Jim finishes doing the can and the shit-shack, washes his hands, and quickly steps to the cottage.

"Did ye wash yer hands?" growls Shaw.

"Yes Mr. Shaw." Jim takes off his coat, shakes it, and hangs it on the coat rack.

"Sit down, supper is ready. Beans tonight lad, sorry for that" murmurs Shaw. The old man serves the bean broth and sits down, closes his eyes, and folds his hands in prayer.

"Preserve me, O God: for in thee do I put my trust. For thou wilt not leave my soul in hell; neither wilt thou suffer thine Holy One to see corruption. Thou wilt shew me the path of life: in thy presence is fullness of joy; at thy right hand there are pleasures for evermore. Thank ye Lord for our meal tonight. Amen."

"Amen," whispers Jim. The two men start to eat their meal. The evening is calm; only the ever present drizzle spoils what would be a starry night.

"Ye've been in ma room today, haven't ye?" utters Shaw in a deep hoarse voice. Jim freezes and swallows the beans quickly.

"Have ye?" bawls the old man. Jim puts the spoon down and looks at Shaw wide eyed.

"No, no, Mr. Shaw, I was doing my chores," answers the boy in a shaky voice. Shaw puts down his spoon, stands up, and limps over to Jim. In a lightning move the old man grabs the boy by the collar and punches him in the mouth. The young man lurches across the kitchen. Shaw grabs him again and issues a second blow to the face. Pots, pans, dishes, fly all over the place. Unrelenting, the old man grabs Jim and slings him like a rag doll across the round table. Jim stands up hurriedly and motions Shaw to stop. The old man is in a rage that Jim has never seen before. Shaw swings a left hook, but this time Jim ducks, and it misses him. He tries to head for the front door, but Shaw grabs him at his shirt and pulls him back. Jim's shirt is ripped apart.

"Ye wee clarty[45] rat! Take this!" Shaw smashes a fist onto Jim's nose and a cracking sound is heard. The blood squirts out of the boy's nose. The old man punches Jim relentlessly blow after

---

[45] dirty

blow in the belly and kidneys. Jim stretches his hand and fetches a large butcher knife from the kitchen counter and points it to Shaw.

"Och! What a man! A knife, so scary! What ye gaunnae dae with it boy! Ye want to stick it in me, dae ye?" hollers Shaw and he takes off his shirt and vest and stands bare chested right in front of Jim.

"Well! Stick it lad!" yells Shaw full chested. Jim holds the knife with both hands and the tip of the knife is inches away from Shaw's belly. The boy feels a rage boiling up in him. He starts to shake uncontrollably.

"WELL, WHAT YE WAITING FOR! STICK IT!" hollers Shaw again. The blood from Jim's mouth and nose drips on his hands. Slowly the young man lowers the knife and drops it on the floor. Shaw turns, picks up a chair, and sits down; he is all sweaty and panting. The boy just stands there.

"Have ye been in ma room?" asks Shaw again.

"Yes Mr. Shaw," answers the boy in a shaky voice. Jim stands there looking at the floor. Shaw pulls out a handkerchief and throws it to the young man.

"Clean yerself," he mutters. Jim dips the handkerchief in the water bowl and puts it on his nose. The blood still streams out. He sits down at the other side of the table.

"Ye know why the rammy[46], dae ye?" asks Shaw still out of breath. Jim slowly nods. "Why?" asks the old man.

"I shouldn't have gone in your room," replies Jim in a low voice.

"Neay lad! That's not the reason Ah gave ye a laldy[47]! Ye lied to me!" roars the old man.

Jim sits quiet holding the handkerchief on his nose.

---

[46] fight
[47] beating

"There's nothing worse than liars. What's a man without his word? NOTHING! Never ever lie to me again. The truth may be bitter, but it is and remains the truth. Ye shouldn't have gone in ma room, but worse than that, you shouldn't lie. Liars are worse than clypes[48]! Don't do that again." Shaw stands up, puts on his shirt and vest, and limps over to Jim. The young man stands up and takes a step back.

"Easy lad, let me take a look at that," utters Shaw. Jim slowly removes the handkerchief. Shaw examines the nose.

"I think it's broken," whispers the old man.

"Sit down lad, I'll help ye with that." The boy slowly sits down. On his way to fetch the medicine box Shaw's glance falls on Jim's bare back.

"Ma Lord, who did that to ye?" asks Shaw overwhelmed. The scars of the many canings at Thebes House look like grotesque carvings on Jim's back. Jim stands up, turns around, and hurries to his room. He slams the door shut. Shaw stands there alone for a minute still in unbelieve of what he saw etched on Jim's back. The old man cleans up the room, washes the pots and dishes, and returns everything to its usual order. On the kitchen counter he sees the butcher knife Jim pointed at him. He puts on his impermeable, grabs the knife, and goes out in the drizzling night. The old man walks across the island to the south end cliffs. He stands at the cliff edge and hurls the knife into the sea. He turns around and looks at the light twirling in the dark. The light beam cuts through the night. Far south he sees the lights of a ship crossing Hell's Mouth. He squats down and peers at the ship. Far away he sees the flashing light of the Duncansby Head lighthouse. What goes through the man's mind is only known to God. There is a very light breeze and the ever present miserable drizzle. The ship silently passes by and the ship lights disappear over the dark

---

[48] snitches

horizon. Only the light of Duncansby Head flashes on and off as if in a silent conversation with the light on Muckle Skerry.

"The Lord is ma Light and salvation — whom shall Ah fear? The Lord is the stronghold of ma life — of whom shall Ah be afraid? Thank ye Lord for cooling ma wrath and restraining ma fists. Thou art ma Light and comfort. Ah live in thy House and Temple. Please, forgive me; for ire is a sin. I shall not ire no more. Ma days of wrath, sorrow, and bitterness are over. Ye ken that ma Lord. Thou guideth ma heart and heid with wisdom to help the lad. Forgive me Lord, forgive me. In thou I trust." Shaw stands up and heads back to the cottage.

XIII

The days are much longer now. It's summer 1951 and Muckle Skerry got a taste of the infamous summer thunderstorms last night. The two towers got hit pretty bad by lightning. The lightning arrestor of the lighthouse was pulverized and that of the foghorn isn't in good shape either. Shaw and Jim are up the lighthouse since five in the morning, no time for breakfast today. The arrestors must be fixed promptly. There will be more thunderstorms this summer. Shaw is working feverishly replacing the thick copper cables on top of the lighthouse roof. It's a dangerous job. The old man is on the roof of the lamp house, the highest point of the lighthouse tower. The new copper cables are heavy, but somehow Shaw manages to have them on the roof and replace the damaged ones. Jim assists him standing on the lamp house balcony. Jim and Shaw are barely on speaking terms after the fight a few weeks ago. The boy does his chores and Shaw does his things. The boy didn't sleep much last night. The violent thunderstorm awoke bad memories. The thunderstorm brought back horrid memories of the London Blitz. Memories of the night his parents died are fresh in his head. They couldn't make it to the Tube[49] and Jim and his parents had to hide in the basement of the building. The rolling thunder reverberates just like the pounding of the bombs and the lightning mimics the explosion flashes. Jim recalls how father desperately tried to help mother out of the rubble when part of the basement roof crashed down. The images of his father grabbing him and making their way out of the basement to seek help for mother flash vividly through his mind.

"Jimmy, Jimmy, stop crying, listen to me. Stay here, wait for me here! Don't move. I'll be right back," the boy recalls his father saying. Father left Jim under the thick concrete slab of the metro station entrance and continued his way to seek for help. The doors to the Tube were already closed. The hellish rain of death and destruction was particularly ferocious that December night. The awful sound of the blaring sirens is fresh in Jim's mind. After that night he never saw his father and mother again. After the bombardment a fireman found Jim curled up at the Tube entrance and brought him to a gathering point.

"Jim!" blurts Shaw from the lamp house roof. The boy snaps out of his ruminating.

"The coil! Tie the rope to the coil!" hollers the old man. Jim does that and Shaw hoists the copper cable coil up.

"Last one lad, almost done!" About thirty minutes later Shaw climbs down and joins Jim on the balcony. He takes off his tool belt and hands it to Jim.

"Now the horn," utters Shaw "that is easier than this." Jim picks up the remaining last two copper cable coils and the two men go down the spiral staircase. It's half past ten in the morning. The

---

[49] the London subway

foghorn cable job was indeed easier. By noon the lightning arrestors of both towers are repaired.

"Let's clean up and get lunch lad," murmurs the old man. The boy doesn't say a word.

It is the usual lunch: shortbread with crowdie[50]. The day is sticky and humid. There is no wind.

"It's gaunnae fog tonight. Prepare the horn for service later," instructs Shaw. Jim just nods.

"Dae ye know why Ah know that?" Jim shakes his head.

"No wind, high humidity, and temperature drop at night; the perfect recipe for fog," answers the lighthouse keeper.

"Thirty years of experience and the right teacher is the key. Auld Banach knew his stuff well. Crabbit auld man but wise he was." Jim reaches over and fetches a piece of short-bread.

"Did Banach beat you up?" asks the boy in a defiant tone. Shaw looks surprised at the young man.

"Och, ye can talk!" snaps Shaw "haven't heard ye for weeks."

"Well, did old Banach beat you?" repeats Jim.

"Neay, we had our differences, but no rammies[51]. Ah've never lied to the man."

"I said I'm sorry. You don't have to keep rubbing it in!"

"And Ah said apologies accepted, but ye're tomb-faced for weeks. Today is the first time ye blether in three weeks. What ye want me to dae? Ah dinnae ken what's gaun in yer heid, lad."

"The beating was not necessary."

"Aye it was, lad. Once a liar, always a liar if ye dinnae get skelped. Ah dinnae want liars in ma house. Ye follow?" Jim remains silent.

---

[50] a type of cheese
[51] fights

"Ye see lad, there's nothing as fragile as trust, and trust comes with truth. Once there ain't no trust is 'cause truth is tampered. Once trust is gaun it seldom returns. Ye're my apprentice lad, Ah need to trust what ye tell me is true and ye need to trust what I tell ye is true. Simple. If Ah doubt yer word or ye doubt ma, ye might as well leave Muckle tomorrow. No use keeping ye here. Trustworthiness is an earned virtue, not a given. Ye follow?"

Jim slowly nods his head.

"You trust me?" inquires Jim in a low voice. Shaw stands up and puts the plate in the wash bowl.

"Ah told ye lad, trustworthiness is an earned virtue. Now, let's gau, there's much work to dae!"

The afternoon passes doing work and chores. After doing the can, Jim steps in the main cottage for supper.

"Did ye wash yer hands?" asks Shaw.

"Yes, Mr. Shaw," is the usual reply.

"Gaud! Got Scotch broth tonight! Ah thought ye may like that." Jim nods and sits down. Shaw serves the broth, say the prayers, and the two men savor their meal heartily. After supper Shaw does the dishes and steps into his room. He rummages for something for a minute and then steps back in the main room holding a bottle.

"Ah dinnae drink, but tonight Ah think is a gaud occasion to have some allasch[52]! Ah know, Ah know, Ah'm breaking the no liquor rule, but once in a lang while must be possible, dinnae ye think so lad?"

"I don't drink alcohol, Mr. Shaw," replies Jim somewhat surprised.

"Ah dinnae either, but tonight is special!" mumbles Shaw.

"What's so special tonight?"

---

[52] A German liquor typical of Leipzig

"Tonight, we drink to the memory of Auld Banach! Today thirty years ago I arrived on Muckle and met the auld Pole; ma teacher for five years before he retired and returned to Poland. Wanted to make bigos for dinner tonight but the cable work took all ma time. Bigos takes time to prepare and therefore Ah made broth instead; easier ye know."

"What happened to Banach after he retired?"

"Ah dinnae ken! Haven't heard from the auld Pole syne[53] the last big war. The Commission said he died during the war in Poland."

"The Commission?"

"Aye, the Northern Lighthouse Commission, ma bosses, or better, our bosses. But let's get cranking on the allasch, shall we?" Shaw fetches two shot glasses and opens the bottle.

"Here, lad, up to the rim!" The old man fills the shot glasses, stands up, hollers "slàinte[54]! to gallus[55] Banach!", and chugs down the allasch in one gulp.

"Och, help ma Boab[56], it burns!" utters Shaw in a hoarse voice. Jim just stares at the shot glass.

"Come on, lad! Drink up!" urges Shaw. The boy takes the shot glass and smells the liquor; his face mangles up.

"One chug, lad!" pushes the old man. Slowly Jim brings the glass to his lips, closes his eyes, and gulps up the liquor. He immediately catches a bout of coughing and his face blushes cherry red.

"What's this thing?" coughs Jim loudly.

"It's German liquor lad. Gaud stuff! Here, give it another shot!" Shaw refills the glasses. Jim waves his hand in rejection.

---

[53] since
[54] Cheers in Gaelic
[55] daring
[56] Goodness Gracious

"Here, one more for the sake of auld Banach." Shaw gulps his second shot down. Jim follows and the coughing resumes.

"Why are you drinking this German stuff? There's plenty of good Scotch whisky around."

"Lang story, frein. Lang story." Shaw crashes down on a chair. The room goes quiet for a minute.

"The allasch Ah get from a frein in Leipzig Germany; Gunther Schtaub is his name. He sends me a bottle of allasch every year and Ah send him a bottle of fine Scotch; been doing that for twenty-five years."

"What for?" inquires Jim. Shaw goes quiet. He pours a shot of allasch and chugs it down. The big man isn't used to alcohol and the strong allasch begins to have its effect.

"It's a lang story, frein," mumbles Shaw. Jim motions the old man to go on. Shaw pours another shot and drinks it. His face is red like an apple.

"What the hell. Ye saw my uniforms in the trunk, didnae ye?"

"Yes Mr. Shaw," responds Jim cautiously.

"Those are of the Great War," murmurs Shaw in a low voice. Jim sits up straight. Shaw chugs down another shot of allasch.

"That's how Ah knew ye've been in ma room."

"How's that Mr. Shaw?"

"The trunk has a tiny seal on it. Ah never open it. That evening Ah found the seal broken. That can be only ye that broke it by opening the trunk." Jim remains silent.

"Ye're not drinking lad!" bawls the old man.

"Ah dinnae drink alone." Jim pours a shot and drinks it. The liquor burns all the way down to his stomach. Shaw follows with a shot.

"Me and ma lads in the Great War captured Corporal Gunther and some more Jerries on the Hindenburg line in September 1918."

"Jerries?" asks Jim curious.

"Well, Jerries, Huns, what we called the Germans in the trenches. Their helmets look like a jerry or chanty, a chamber pot. Ye know what ye piss in at night." The boy smiles and nods.

"Ah got acquainted with the poor Hun when we escorted them to the back of the line. He spoke pretty gaud English. He asked me for a fag[57] and Ah gave him one. The poor lad was scared out of his socks. Who wasn't." Shaw goes silent and his gaze turns hazy: as if looking at a ghost.

"What happened then Mr. Shaw?" asks Jim warily.

"He showed me pictures of his wife and two little daughters. He was afraid we're gaunnae shoot them. He shook like a leaf. He and his comrades were all shook up. We gave them a fair laldy the night before." Shaw goes silent and tears well up in his eyes.

"Ah dinnae want to talk about this lad. It's past many years ago. No use bringing it up now. Ah never told anybody this." He pours himself another shot of allasch.

"I want to know. I think it is really important," replies Jim in a firm tone. Shaw looks at him.

"It's too hard lad. Ye'll never understand."

"Oh, no, no, try me Mr. Shaw. I understand more than you think!"

After a pause Shaw continues: "Gunther asked me point blank if we're gaunnae shoot them. I remember he was peely-wally[58]. Ah told him neay; we're escorting them to a temporary prison camp. He didnae believe me. His officers told

---

[57] cigarette
[58] pale

them that we Scots are butchers and dae not take prisoners. Ah told him that's havers. We're no animals. Ah remember saying to him that he's a lucky bastart; his war is over. He smiled and the shaking got less. I got to know Gunther better in the prison camp before they were taken away. It's there that we promised each other that if we survived the war Ah will send him a bottle of Scotch every September and he'll send me a bottle of allasch the same month. He kept his word for twenty-five years and Ah kept ma word. The last bottle of allasch Ah received seven years ago. Ah think he died in the last big war. We never wrote letters; just send bottles."

"Tell me about the war, Mr. Shaw," asks Jim excited.

"Neay, lad, the allasch has gaun to ma heid. It's no gaud talking about that. It's past; let the past be past."

"Please, Mr. Shaw, it is important I know about it," implores the young man.

"Neay, lad, weather is cooling down. The fog will roll in soon. Go start the horn. Ah'll get the light." Shaw stands up, puts his jacket on and steps outside. The image of the old man's eyes is printed in Jim's mind. He could feel the sadness, anguish, and horror in his gaze. Submerged in thought the boy steps outside and heads to the south tower. A few minutes later the south tower beast is heard belching its loud and horrid sound. The north tower light goes on and Muckle Skerry lighthouse is ready for the coming foggy night. The 'beast' will be belching the whole night.

Stepping inside the main cottage, Jim sees a sliver of light under Shaw's bedroom door. The man has retired for the night. A crackly wailing sound protrudes from the old man's quarters. It's the bagpipe. In between the blurting of the horn, the sweet and soft bagpipe tones of the song 'Amazing Grace' is heard. Shaw plays the pipe with such care and tenderness. Jim stands in the main room and savors the melancholy of the tune. The belching beast doesn't bother him. The song ends and the crackly wailing returns as Shaw puts the instrument away. The sliver of light under Shaw's door goes dark and only the foghorn intermittently interrupts the deep silence. Jim blows out the petrol lamps and goes to bed. Another day on Muckle Skerry passes by.

XIV

"Don't forget us, Jim" whispers a child's voice.
"Don't forget us," it whispers again. Jim wakes up and looks at the clock; it is one thirty in the morning. The foghorn blares its loud burp sound intermittently.

"Don't forget us, Jim," whispers a kid's voice followed by a soft but clear sobbing. Jim jumps out of bed and lights a petrol lamp. The sobbing comes from the main room. Slowly, lamp in hand, Jim cracks open the door to the main room, the soft weeping stops. He enters the main room and looks around: nothing unusual. The boy lights a couple of lamps and looks around.

"What are ye gaunnae dae with the boy," utters a soft female voice coming from Shaw's room. Jim freezes up. '*What the hell is going on*' ponders Jim.

"Gau away," replies Shaw. Jim tip toes to the old man's bedroom door and eavesdrops. The slit underneath Shaw's door is dark.

"Don't forget us," whispers a child's voice from Jim's room. Jim slowly turns around and silently goes to his room; there is nothing.

"Ye must dae something," utters the female voice softly.

"Gau away," answers Shaw again. Jim's heart is now in overdrive and sweat breaks out on his forehead. Slowly he steps to Shaw's room and knocks softly on the door.

"Mr. Shaw?" utters Jim quietly, "Mr. Shaw?" The slit under the door shows a sliver of light. He hears movement in Shaw's room and a few seconds later the old man opens the door.

"Well, lad, what's gaun on? Ye ken what hour is?" grumbles Shaw with a sleepy face.

"I heard a woman's voice coming from your room Mr. Shaw," utters Jim nervously. Shaw looks at him sardonically, "ye're having wet dreams lad?" chuckles Shaw.

"No, no, Mr. Shaw, really, I also heard a child weeping in here, the main room."

"Ye're sleepwalking lad, gau back to bed!" mumbles Shaw annoyed.

"No, Mr. Shaw I'm wide awake!"

"Gau to bed! Lang day tomorrow," Shaw slams the door shut. The horn blurts again. Jim stands there and looks around. He gets the creeps and hurriedly blows out the lamps in the room and goes into his bedroom. He sits at the edge of the bed and looks at himself in the mirror hanging opposite to him.

"I'm not asleep," he mutters. The boy looks out of the window; the fog is not dense, but visibility is poor. The tower light flashes by with a constant frequency. Jim lies down but sleep is out of the question.

The day is warm and humid. Shaw disassembled the engine driving the rotating mirror and instructs Jim to put it back together while identifying each part by name and function. The engine room at the top of the tower is small and the diesel smell suffocating. Jim did his studies and the reassembling of the engine goes well. Shaw is impressed.

"See there lad, all goes well if ye put time into it. Ye did better than Ah did with auld Banach!" chuckles Shaw. Jim wipes off the mix of grease and sweat from his hands. "Now, let's see what ye did," bawls Shaw hoarsely. He opens the main fuel valve, waits a minute, and then cranks up the engine. It starts without a problem and the hellish noise fills up the small room.

"Braw!" yells the old man smiling. Shaw puts two fingers on the engine block and closes his eyes. After a minute or so, he smiles and yells again "braw!" With a quick head motion Shaw indicates to Jim that it's time to move out. He shuts down the engine and the noise dies out.

"Ye did well, lad. Next are the lamp and the gearbox. The lamp is tricky. Ye'll need some coaching at that. It's the heart of all we dae. Ye must know the lamp well."

"I heard you answer the woman last night," asserts Jim quietly.

"Och, lad, ye're still on that story? Ye'd an awry dream, that's all."

"Why did the apprentice before me leave in such a hurry?"

"Och, that Jessie! He feart[59] his own shadow," scoffs Shaw. "He couldn't handle the pressure, Ah guess."

"And the one that drowned?" inquires Jim uneasily.

"The swells knocked him off the cliff. Told him not to mess with the swells. He got too close, poor lad." The two men get out of the tower and Shaw closes the door.

"Who's the woman in the portrait?" inquires Jim cautiously.

"That's none of yer business," replies Shaw immediately.

"I did hear the voices last night. I wasn't sleepwalking."

"Give it a shoogle[60], will ye!" snarls Shaw.

In the late afternoon, dark clouds gather at the western horizon. Another thunderstorm approaches. Jim's mind is rushing in hyper drive. '*The voices and the weeping were real*!' Far away the

---

[59] afraid, afraid of, fears
[60] shake

echoes of thunder are heard, and the wind slowly picks up. Jim does the can job in a hurry and rushes to the cottage.

"Did ye wash yer hands?" blurts the old man as usual.

"Yes Mr. Shaw."

"It's gaunnae be aglae[61] tonight. Hope the towers dinnae get a laldy. We ran out of cable," mumbles Shaw. He folds his hands, shuts his eyes, and says the prayers. Supper is the usual potatoes and spinach.

"Is the woman in the portrait your wife?" asks Jim softly. Shaw puts down his spoon and looks with piercing eyes at Jim.

"Told ye none of yer business!"

"I heard you talk to a woman last night." Jim pushes the envelope. Shaw leans back and crosses his arms.

"Ye're not believing the galoot[62] bogle[63] stories of auld Reid Lieutenant Blake told ye, dae ye?" mocks Shaw.

"My predecessor experienced something. He left scared crazy. I heard what I heard last night, and I wasn't sleeping!" retorts Jim firmly.

"Havers! Yer predecessor was an eejit! Ye're not an eejit. Dinnae be a wee scunner[64]!"

Jim finishes the potato grub, stands up, and washes his plate. A loud thunderclap crashes in. Shaw sits straight up.

"Oh Lord, we're up for a pounding tonight." The wind whistles loudly and the rain starts to pour down. The cottage roof cracks slightly. Shaw stands up, returns the food to the pot, and grabs his pipe.

"Ah never merrit[65]," utters the old man calmly.

---

[61] ugly
[62] stupid
[63] phantom
[64] whiner
[65] married

"Why not?" asks Jim. Shaw lights the pipe, sits down, and leans back dreamy faced.

"The woman in the portrait is Anne Duncan," utters Shaw softly. Jim sits down.

"She was ma fiancée a lang time ago; never merrit her."

"Did she die?"

"Neay, she merrit a lad from Glasgow."

"She's really pretty," comments Jim.

"Aye she is," replies Shaw and goes into a deep silence.

"You still love her?" inquires Jim curious. Shaw remains silent.

"Why did she marry the man from Glasgow?"

After a long silence Shaw replies,

"Ah was in the trenches. It was the end of the summer of 1917. Miserable day it was. The rain poured down and me and ma lads were drookit[66]. We were up to our knees in clarty mud. Ah got a letter from her. She said in the letter she couldn't wait no more. She met this Glasgow lad in Inverness. All the incoming names of the deid and missing made her anxious. She said she couldn't handle it no more 'cause chances are that Ah may not return. Ah was 37 years of age and she 35. She was afraid to be too old to get children. That was the worst day for me. By the time the war ended, and Ah got hame[67] she was merrit with a bairn[68]. She was probably right, at that time Ah didnae ken if Ah was gaun back hame either."

"Did you see her after the war?"

"Neay. Didnae want to affect her life. She merrit already; what's the use." A loud thunderclap cracks close by and Jim and Shaw make a little jump in their chairs.

---

[66] soaking wet
[67] home
[68] child

"Hoots!" bawls Shaw "we're gaunnae get a skelping!" The whistle of the wind turns into a howl.

"She's affecting your life," utters Jim "bet you she doesn't have your picture beside her bed." Shaw stands up, gives Jim the finger, and retires to his room.

"The horn, Mr. Shaw, do I have to start the foghorn!" hollers Jim.

"Neay! No fog! Too much wind! Gau to yer scratcher[69] and dinnae dream havers tonight!" Shaw slams the bedroom door shut.

XV

It is mid-August and the morning is clammy and hot. Shaw boarded Hope and departed to John o' Groats to do the messages. Jim gave him a letter to post for him to his orphan roommates in Aberdeen.

Muckle Skerry, Wednesday, August 15th, 1951
Dear Herbert,
I hope all is well with you and the guys. I've learned a lot about the lighthouse and how to handle it. The weather is, as usual, quite nasty. We've had a number of heavy thunder storms this summer. They can be really scary. Mr. Shaw is a Great War hero. I saw his uniforms and medals. We had a scuffle one night, but all is well now. I saw his gun and rifle too. They are quite heavy. Perhaps, if I ask nicely he will teach me how to use them. However, in general, it is quite a bore here. I'm sick of the never ending mundane chores. I want to leave this place as soon as I get a reasonable chance. Furthermore, I think the place spooks. One night

---

[69] bed

I heard strange children voices and the voice of a woman. There are no children or women on Muckle. Shaw assures me that I was sleepwalking, but I know I wasn't. It can be quite hairy and spooky here. It is spookier than Thebes House. I hope you and the guys are doing well. Overall, Mr. Shaw treats me well and sometimes he cooks these delicious dishes. In any case, the food is better than in Thebes House. Give the Wobbs hell for me will you? Please, feel free to read this letter to Orville and Norman and give them my best regards for me.

Your friend, sincerely, Jimmy.

Jim struggles to unlock the door. Shaw locked his bedroom door before leaving to Groats. Jim knows he's risking another beating, but he must take a better look around in the room. The strange voices and the story of his predecessors is haunting him. He intuitively feels that the answers to his questions lay beyond the locked door. He fidgets with a crooked nail and a pincer in the door lock. *"Clack!"* sounds the lock; he's got it. Lock picking is one of the clandestine skills he learned at the Thebes House. He sprints out of the cottage, climbs the south tower, and peers to the southern sea to make sure Shaw left. Hope is not there. He scans Hell's Mouth with the binoculars and spots Hope heading to Groats.

"Good!" yelps Jim and he rushes back in.

The bedroom door squeaks open, and Jim enters Shaw's room. The bed is squarely made up. Jim doesn't touch the trunk or the wardrobe. He picks up the portrait and takes a good look at the woman holding a rose. She's indeed very pretty. Her smile has something disobedient and mischievous. Her eyes have this strange twinkle. Jim puts the portrait back on the night table and goes to the bookcase. He browses and rummages through it. He finds a series of five books with the letters 'W.B.' on the cover. He pulls one out of the bookcase and opens it. It's handwritten and the handwriting is clearly old school. The language is unknown to Jim but here and there are parts written in English. Each page has a date on it. It is either a diary or logbook. The letters 'W.B.' stand for Wladyslaw Banach, Shaw's teacher and former lighthouse keeper. Jim browses through the book and reads the bits and pieces written in English.

Had to nail the cross at the door; she wanted to come in.

Light went out! Devil is back.

16th of April 1899. The Vincent crashed at the south end. Thank the all merciful God that all hands got dry. She lured the poor lads badly.

Jim pulls the second book out of the bookcase and leaf's through it.

17th August 1903, bad storm. The wretched giggle drives me crazy.

Light went out. Struggled to put back on. Hands were heavy. The bitch had me good.

Burns hanged himself. Not happening to me.

23rd March 1908. The horn wouldn't turn off. Tampered. The hand of the devil.

Jim slams the book shut. He shoves the books back into the bookcase. His mind is blank. A slow chill creeps up his spine. However, his nosiness gets a firmer grip on him. He pulls out the third book.

Found a body washed up in Narrow cove. All mangled, swollen and blue. Had a crucifix clenched in hand. Horrible face. Poor lad; she had him good.

The tombstone was toppled. Put it back. They are restless.

Whole month of straight fog. This is not weather; it is witchcraft!

They got in. The Lord was with me.

Jim closes the book and grabs the fifth one.

12th of May, 1921. Brave man, Lewis. The bitch found her match. The war made this man iron.

Fire in the barn. Put it out but barn useless. Poor Margarethe is dead. The slut from hell just giggled standing in the courtyard corner.
13th of September, 1925. Shaw is ready.

Jim read enough. He puts the book back in the bookcase. Leaves the room and locks the door.

Shaw arrives back at Muckle in the late afternoon. The number of seagulls flying around is extra-ordinary. The cackling and squealing is deafening. Jim gives Shaw a hand with storing the provisions. After that, the boy follows up doing the can. Shaw prepares dinner.

"Did ye wash yer hands?" Jim sits down at the table and gives his usual everyday answer.

"Screwed up yer plans, didnae Ah?" utters Shaw mockingly.

"What plans," asks Jim.

"The door was locked. Ye didnae expect that, did ye?" chuckles Shaw. Jim puts the crooked nail and the pincer on the table.

"Lock picking, my specialty!" gloats Jim. Shaw drops the spoon and his face turns red like a cherry.

"Before you beat me up; this time I didn't lie. Yes, I went in your room." Jim stands up and starts taking off his shirt readying himself for the scuffle. Shaw stands there red faced and biting his tongue. He picks up the spoon and takes a deep breath.

"Put yer shirt on. Ah'm not gaunnae waste ma time on ye." The boy puts on his shirt and sits down. In a dry voice Jim says, "You lied to me." Shaw stops the stirring.

"Ye calling me a liar!" blurts the old man.

"YES!" replies Jim. The red hue returns on Shaw's face. "I read Banach's logbook!" bawls Jim.

"Och, ye read Polish now, genius!" scoffs Shaw.

"I read the bits in English."

"So?" rebukes the old man.

"Who is she?" demands Jim.

"She who?" answers Shaw.

"The one Banach writes about; the bitch, the devil!" blurts Jim.

"Och, lad, dinnae be an eejit! Auld Banach was very superstitious. Ye know, Catholicism brings with it a lot of spooks and demons. All havers, ma lad."

"You're a Catholic, aren't you?"

"Ye see a crucifix in this house?" answers Shaw immediately.

"No."

"Don't ask galoot questions then!" Jim leans back and puts his hands on his face.

"Auld Banach was very superstitious. He believed in witches, devils, and demons. All havers! The only demons are us. Ah saw plenty of them in the war and they were all flesh and blood just like ye and Ah. There are no phantoms here. It's all in yer mind, lad."

"Who was Burns?" inquires Jim abruptly.

"Burns was the keeper before Banach," answers Shaw laconically.

"He hanged himself," bawls Jim.

"People hang themselves every day," rebukes Shaw stoically.

"Banach mentions you in the last book. The barn fire, what happened?"

"Ah forgot a lit oil lamp. The straw caught fire. We put it out. The cow died."

"Margarethe?" asks Jim.

"Aye. All cows on Muckle are called Margarethe or Maggy. Keeps the tradition."

"Banach mentions in many passages a witch or bitch. What does he mean?"

"Told ye lad, the man was auld and superstitious. Gaud man but saw bogles everywhere. It was all in his mind. Dinnae let that bother ye."

"But I heard the woman's voice that night," utters Jim anxiously.

"Ye were sleepwalking lad. Let gau!" Jim goes into a deep silence.

"He writes that the war made you of steel and that she met her match with you."

"The auld man is delirious. He drank a lot. Dinnae worry about his babbling."

"Have you read his logs?" asks Jim worried.

"Aye. After he left Muckle. Amusing stuff. Dinnae read Polish but read the English bits. Nice handwriting, dinnae ye think so? The auld man should have been a writer, not a keeper!"

An awkward feeling enters Jim's gut. Banach lived on Muckle for thirty years. He can't believe that Banach wrote nonsense in his logs all those years.

"You're not telling me the truth," murmurs Jim.

"What truth? Ah've just told ye the truth. Banach was a gaud man, liked his Scotch, staunch Catholic, and was superstitious. What else ye want me to tell ye? Now, let's eat." Shaw scoops up the food and puts the plates on the table. He sits down, folds his hands, and shuts his eyes.

"The Lord is ma Light and salvation — whom shall Ah fear? The Lord is the stronghold of ma life — of whom shall Ah be afraid? One thing Ah ask from the Lord, this only Ah seek: that Ah may dwell in the house of the Lord all the days of ma life, to gaze on the beauty of the Lord and to seek him in his temple. Thank ye Lord for our meal tonight. Amen."

"Amen," whispers Jim. They silently consume their meal.

XVI

September 11th, 1951. Shaw and Jim are doing maintenance work on the lamp assembly of the lighthouse. In a well-organized and meticulous way Shaw teaches and instructs Jim the peculiar technical details of the lamp and the lamp fuel system. Jim pays close attention to every move Shaw does and takes notes. He knows that the lamp is at the core of their purpose for being on Muckle Skerry. Shaw almost brainwashes Jim about the importance of the light being on when it must be on without failing; *'lives are at stake'* as Shaw puts it. At first glance, the lamp assembly looks simple, but in reality, it takes certain skill and knowhow to operate and maintain in top shape. Shaw proves to be a master at this, and he passionately passes his skills and knowledge over to Jim. Although Jim loathes being on Muckle, he is silently enjoying the master class in lighthouse lamp anatomy and maintenance. Since seven in the morning Jim and the old man disassembled, inspected, cleaned, and polished every part of the lamp. Shaw treats the assembly with an almost holy reverence. Everything must be perfect. At around three o'clock in the afternoon the lamp job is completed. Shaw pumps the kerosene mist-generator up and signals to Jim to light the pilot wick. A strange hissing sound is produced, and the three large bulbs start to glow red and about a minute later they flash into a fierce bright white light. Shaw smiles broadly as if in love with the contraption.

"Ain't that bonnie?" he mumbles "ma wee bairn is clean and sparkling." Shaw claps his hands and does a little Scottish dance. Jim never saw him this ecstatic.

After supper Jim discovers part of the reason why Shaw is so joyous; it's his birthday. Shaw pops up a brand-new bottle of allasch and opens it. He pours the allasch in the shot glasses and swigs the 'German fire water' down.

"Hoots! That burns! Drink up lad, slàinte!" hollers the old man full chested. Jim takes his time drinking the liquor.

"I heard you playing the pipes. I didn't know you're a piper," comments Jim.

"Och, aye!" yelps Shaw and rushes to his bedroom. The intermittent squeals of the bagpipe is heard when Shaw unpacks the instrument. The loud notes of *Scotland the Brave* fill the cottage and Shaw marches out the bedroom bagpipe under arm and playing away. He trudges around the table bagpipe full blast. Jim enjoys both sound and view. Shaw is happy like a puppy with a fresh bone. The old man plays the song to completion, carefully places the bagpipe on a chair, and sits down. A silent sadness descends on his face. He sits there and stares at the instrument for a few seconds.

"Brings up many auld memories," murmurs Shaw softly. Jim remains still. The old man picks up the bagpipe and puts it on his lap. The instrument utters a soft moan as if lamenting something.

"You were a piper in the army?" asks Jim prudently. Shaw nods his head.

"Aye, lad, Ah played ma frein on many times during the war, happy occasions and sad occasions. All of them are etched in ma heid. They won't leave." Shaw hits another shot of allasch. He caresses the instrument as if a kitten.

"Tell me about the war Mr. Shaw." The old man fills the shot glasses up.

"Drink up lad!" he bawls. Jim carefully consumes the liquor. The hangover of the last allasch deluge is fresh in his mind. Shaw puts the bagpipe on the chair and lights his smoking pipe.

"War is a nasty business ma frein. Ah've lived through four in ma life; the last is raging right now, Korea. The first two Ah've fought." Jim sits straight up.

"Two Mr. Shaw?" The old man takes a drag and leans back.

"Aye, South Africa and the Great One: filthy business." Jim fills the shot glasses.

"South Africa?" the boy asks curiously.

"Aye, the Boers, sneaky bastarts, they hunted us down like rats. Ah was 17 when Ah volunteered to go to Africa. Didnae ken what Ah was doing. Ye know, Ah was young and a gowk[70]! Bonnie land but treacherous. The Boers knew every nick and cranny; we were like sitting ducks. Lost many gaud lads there. Got to know the blacks, braw people. Wise people and brave. It's their land, ye know. White fighting white for king and country. We had nothing to dae there. The blacks treated me well 'cause Ah gave them respect. Somehow Ah knew Ah didnae belong there. The blacks suffered horribly. We had these camps, ye know. The poor people starved to deid. They had no blame for what's gaun on, but they paid the price. We finally gained control of the situation in 1901, but by then many paid the price. The Black Watch are professionals. We did what we had to dae. We hunted the Boer bastarts and killed them. It was aglae." Shaw goes silent. Jim pours the allasch again. Shaw silently chugs it down.

"Tell me about the Great War" asks the young man. Shaw squints and puts the glass down.

---

[70] fool

"The Boer war was a stroll compared to the Big One. Ma battalion landed in L 'Havre in August 1914 and the keech started flying around soon after. We were the first of the British to put foot in France. We were marched to the front immediately. By then Ah was a professional soldier, Ah knew ma stuff. Nonetheless, no one was prepared for what was coming. We marched into Mons and everything looked gaud. It's gaunnae be a short war everybody thought. But then the Jerries launched their attack. We got a nasty skelping. We had a fighting retreat, but it was aglae." Shaw goes silent; tears well up in his eyes. Jim feels his pain and remains quiet.

"What happened then?" asks Jim.

Shaw looks at him, "Mons, Marne, Somme, Messines, Polygon Wood, Passchendaele, all bloody places Ah rather forget. They are nailed in ma heid. Poelcapelle is one of those. Ah wasn't in Poelcapelle. Auld McGraw was. Ye met him in Groats. It's too hard to tell these stories lad. Ah never told anyone before. Ah dinnae ken why Ah'm telling ye now. Ah guess it must be told for young lads like ye not to dae the same. Ah have something for ye." Shaw goes in his room and comes back with a piece of paper. He hands it to Jim.

"Ah ain't a writer, but this is how it feels." The paper has a poem on it. Jim reads it.

When the guns went silent

The guns are now quiet.
Strange is the silence.
Ah think Ah hear birds sing
For the first time in years.

Still in the mud they lyeth;
Eyes shut and tired of violence.
Blood and death is one thing,
But the stench! That, no one bears.

It seems the butchery stopped.
Silent is it all; dark and strange.
From bullets to champagne popped;
So stark, so deranged.

The guns are now quiet.
And here ma freins lyeth
In Flanders' mud;
Soaked in young men's blood.

Some got mangled,
Some just disappeared.
Some had their spirit strangled,
And some turned utterly weird.

To call ma home a trench,
And a rat ma pet,
Is now high mark of the bench.
So much for life and all of that.

So, the guns are quiet now.
The war seems over and done.
It's just that Ah dinnae know how
To leave behind ma Brothers long gone.

"It all feels like a waste," utters Shaw in a crackly voice.

"No, no, it was not!" yelps Jim. The old man stands up, grabs the bagpipe, and goes to his room. Jim reads the poem again. Shaw comes back and sits down.

"Tell me about the scars on yer back" utters the old man calmly. Jim looks at him wide eyed.

"The words in the writing tell it all about ma war. Now ye tell me about the scars on yer back, who did that to ye?" Jim stands up and heads to his room. Shaw grabs the boy's arm firmly.

"Neay frein, Ah told ye ma war, now ye tell me yers! Sit doon!" demands Shaw adamantly. Jim sits down and immediately shrouds himself in silence. Shaw pours another shot of allasch. The liquor is having its effect on him.

"The scars are bad," utters the old man. "Who did that to ye?" The boy is silent like a tomb. He stares to the floor as if looking into an abyss.

"At least we could fight back," murmurs Shaw "did the nuns dae that?" Jim shakes his head.

"The priests did," utters the boy softly. "Why?" inquires the old man. After a short silence Jim responds, "because they're hypocrites." Shaw stands up and grabs his pipe.

"What have ye done to deserve such laldy?"

"I saw and said things I shouldn't have," mumbles Jim and tears well up in his eyes. Shaw lights the pipe and walks around agitated.

"The biggest lie of all are the priests and the Wobbs. They pretend to serve God, but they only serve themselves. They're wolves dressed in sheep skin. Your god let innocents suffer and die. I've seen it; I was there." Shaw hits another shot of allasch and his face progressively turns redder.

"What have they done?" asks the old man disturbed. After a brief silence Jim responds in a barely audible voice.

"They rape children. They starve us as punishment. They humiliate us. They punish us for the pettiest things. The Wobbs and the priests have sex. They violate sacred confession. They lock us up for days in dark catacombs." Jim's hate radiates from his eyes and is clearly palpable from his tone of voice. Shaw can't believe what he's hearing.

"A friend of my took her life. She was raped many times by a priest. She couldn't live with the shame. I tried to talk her out of it. She hung herself. Her body just disappeared." The tears stream down Jim's face. His ire and hate are at a boiling point. Shaw stands there as if paralyzed.

"The scars are the result of bamboo canings. The priests caned me several times. I passed out every time and woke up in the catacombs smeared in blood. The Wobbs knew what was happening but they kept quiet, including Mother Agnes. Many of them are nothing more than the priest's whores. I and my friends survived because we could lie our way out of many punishable situations. I learned to deceive from the master deceivers: the priests and Wobbs." Shaw sits down; his mind is in total disbelieve.

"Try to let gau, lad. The hate will kill ye." Jim jumps up, looks the old man straight in the eyes, and hollers a loud growl drenched in pain. The boy's eyes are blood red and the hate radiates out of them.

"I've been trying to let go all my life! Many took their own life because they couldn't handle it no more. What kept me going is revenge: the day I see the hypocrites pay for their sins!"

"Keep the Light and ye shall be set free," utters Shaw calmly.

"The light, the stupid light, what does it have to do with this!" blurts Jim.

"Everything," replies the old man. Jim looks at him in disbelieve.

"Did you hear what I just told you?" bawls the young man in a rage.

"If there is a god, a god of good and mercy, why does he allow such evil in a house that's supposed to serve him? Why does he allow innocents to suffer and die? Why doesn't he punish the real evil doers? All of this god and Jesus stuff is nonsense, a scheme to keep the meek stupid!" Jim crashes down on the chair. Shaw puts his pipe aside and leans forward.

"Ye remember the sheep's eyes and squeals before Ah slaughtered it?" asks Shaw with an intense look on his face.

Jim nods, "it doesn't leave my mind."

"Ah've seen many eyes like that: not of sheep but of men. The Great War wasn't about shelling and shooting from trench to trench. Trench raids were men to men fighting and killing each other with whatever you had in yer hands." Shaw's eyes are fierce.

"That wild stare of fear, screams, and moans of men dying grips yer heid. Gun, bayonet, shovel, helmet, whatever it took to kill Ah used. The rifle and gun ye saw in ma room are drenched in blood. They took many Hun lives either with a bullet or bayonet. 'Fix bayonets' was for me the most fearsome order. Ah could smell the fear, ma own and ma lads, while waiting for the whistle to go over the top[71]. Ye know what fear smells like? It smells like sweat, piss, and keech. Anyone who says he wasn't scared to go over the top is a clarty liar. Once over the top, Ah became a beast, a savage! Ma heid went into a blank and all Ah thought of is for me and ma lads to survive. Ah can't put it in words lad. The sudden rain of blood when a lad is blown to pieces next to ye, the body parts flying around, pieces of brains on yer uniform, the screams, the moans, the stench, there are no words to express the horror. When the armistice commenced, eleven o'clock in the morning on November the eleventh 1918, an eerie silence fell over the whole

---

[71] step out of the trench into no man's land to attack the enemy

line; Ah was an empty shell of a man. Ah felt nothing. Ah was a lost soul and so were many of ma lads who made it back alive. Ye see this." Shaw drops his pants and shows Jim his right thigh. There is a fair chunk of flesh missing.

"Passchendaele 1917, a machine gun bullet ripped through ma leg; and see this." Shaw takes off his vest and shirt and shows me a scar on his left shoulder.

"Jerry sniper at the Somme; they were gaud the bastarts. A miracle he missed ma heid. A wounded soldier is more of a burden than a deid one, Ah guess." Shaw puts his pants, shirt, and vest back on. Jim is horrified.

"Ye see ma frein, when Ah returned hame Ah wandered about the streets of Edinburgh for nearly two years. There were no jobs. People wouldn't believe the horrors of the war. Folks were tired of war and all they wanted is to go on with their life. Many lads took their life after the Great War: the loneliness, bitterness, and horror got a hold of them. This job saved ma life." Shaw sits down and goes silent.

"Why?" asks Jim softly.

"Ah was like ye lad, full of hate, ire, and self-pity. Ah saw the add in a newspaper and applied. The Northern Lighthouse Commission was looking for a lighthouse keeper apprentice for Muckle Skerry. Ah guess Muckle is so desolated that nobody was interested. Ah got the job and met auld Banach. He was on Muckle twenty-five years when Ah arrived. Banach was a gaud man. He taught me to see the Light. He liked his Scotch, but he was a wise auld man. One stormy night he told me that for every night the light is on, each ship that passes through Hell's Mouth is safe. The light saves lives. That's why the light must be on and stay on every night and in foul weather; it saves lives. Every ship that passes Hell's Mouth safely and guided by the light are lives saved. Every life saved brings me deliverance for every life Ah took in the wars.

The light cleans ma soul of sin and ma hands of blood. That's why it must be lit every night. It's ma sole purpose on Muckle. Ah have taken lives in the wars and now Ah've dedicated ma life to save lives in Hell's Mouth waters by keeping the Light. Ma soul and heart were once dark and full of hate lad. The Light taught me to let gau and serve it, for only gaud comes from the Light. Let gau, lad, and the Light will set ye free."

Jim puts his hands on his face and sobs loudly. Shaw stands up, walks over to the boy, helps him up, and brings the weeping young man to his bedroom.

"Let it out lad. It's the only way to get rid of the fester." The old man blows out the kerosene lamp, leaves Jim's room, and closes the door. He takes a last shot of allasch, blows out the lamps, and retires to his room. It's the first time Shaw told his story. Somehow, he feels relieved; their names liveth for evermore.

XVII

As always, the entrance hall of Thebes House is scantily lit. The big crucifix with Jesus is surrounded by candles and a kneeled Wobb prays in front of the crucifix. Jim can hear the Wobb's prayer. That voice is familiar to Jim. Slowly he approaches the praying nun from behind. He knows that voice.

"Excuse me Sister," whispers Jim prudently. The nun stops her prayers, does the sign of the cross, stands up and turns. Her face is hidden in the shadows. Jim takes a few steps closer to get a better look at her face. His eyes grow big.

"Hullo Jimmy, I'm Sister Anne."

The young lad jumps out of bed and trips over the chair. The Wobb's face is that of the woman in the portrait: Anne Duncan. Jim lights a lamp. His hands are shaking. The voice is the same voice he heard that night coming from Shaw's quarters. The foghorn blurts its disgusting sound. It's end September and the autumn fog start rolling in. Jim sits down and tries to calm himself. *This was definitely a dream, but that other night was no dream*' thinks Jim. The boy puts on his pants and vest and goes into the main room. It's three o'clock in the morning. He lights some oil lamps, pours a cup of milk, and sits down at the round table. He looks at the slit underneath Shaw's bedroom door. It's dark; Shaw is sleeping. The light of the lighthouse flashes periodically through the kitchen window. The holler of the foghorn rips through the silent night. The fog isn't dense. Jim finishes drinking the milk, puts on his trench coat, and steps outside. Standing in the foggy courtyard he hears Maggy mooing in the barn. Jim steps over to the barn. Just when he's going to open the barn door Maggy utters a loud moo and he hears a strange giggle coming from inside the barn. Jim freezes up. It sounds like a kid's snigger. Maggy moos again but this time in a more anxious tone as if something is bothering her. The boy slides the barn door open and sticks the oil lamp inside. The sheep and pigs are in their stalls, the chickens are asleep on the roof beams, and Maggy looks at Jim. Everything looks okay. Suddenly Jim hears the giggling coming from outside the barn. His heart pounds like the engine drive of the tower light mirror. He steps outside and catches a glimpse of a shadow moving through the fog near the provision room. The shivers hit Jim bad, and he closes the barn and rushes back to the main cottage. Once inside, he lights more oil lamps. The low pitch holler of the horn gives him the creeps. '*There is something out there, but what?*' Jim peers into the courtyard from the front window. Suddenly something slams into the window and a loud squeal is heard. A large seagull flaps its wings and pecks on the window glass. As sudden as it appeared, the seagull disappears squealing loudly. *'Gulls don't fly at night'* reasons Jim. *'Is it that what I saw moving in the fog?'* The young man sits in the main room till Shaw wakes up.

"Ye're up early lad. Had a gaud sleep?" mumbles Shaw while preparing coffee and breakfast.

"I heard giggles in the barn Mr. Shaw, and shadows moving in the fog. A large seagull crashed into the front window." Jim goes to the front windows and shows Shaw two scratch marks in the glass. Shaw shakes his head and smiles.

"Awry dreams again, lad?" chuckles the old man.

"Oh no, I was wide awake Mr. Shaw. I even had a cup of milk," utters Jim nervously. "The galoot birds get hoachin' when they're in heat; they dinnae sleep, just hoochie-hoochie, ye know," sniggers Shaw.

"Come, let's have breakfast. The Guards are coming today, isn't it?"

"Yes Mr. Shaw, they confirmed by radio yesterday."

"Gaud! Need the fuel! At least the radio contraption is gaud for something," blurts the old man. "What were ye doing at the barn lad?"

"I couldn't sleep; had a bad dream. I heard Maggy mooing nervously and went to look if she is okay. It's then when I heard the giggles, a kid giggling."

"Could be the gulls. They make strange noises when doing their hoochie."

"The giggles came from within the barn," assures Jim.

"Could be the chickens," murmurs Shaw with a mouth full of short-bread.

"No Mr. Shaw, I heard a kid giggle, not seagulls or chickens" affirms Jim upset. Shaw stands up, puts his plate in the wash bowl, drinks up his coffee, shrugs, grabs his coat, and steps outside. The fog is still out there. The old man opens the barn and drives the animals out. It is still dark. There isn't a gull around. Only the blurting noise of the horn fills the courtyard.

At about nine in the morning, Jim shuts down the foghorn. The fog has lifted and there is finally some quiet. Far away a different horn blurts. Jim hurries up the south tower and peers through the binoculars. It's the H.M.C.G. Sparrow on its way to Muckle.

The Sparrow throws anchor and the loading and unloading activities are in full swing. Lieutenant Blake comes on shore and as usual Shaw invites him for a cup of coffee. Blake lights a cigarette and turns to Jim.

"You see, chap, how easy it is to have a radio station. It is old Shaw here that resisted for years having a radio located on Muckle," cajoles the Lieutenant. Shaw doesn't heed Blake's tongue-in-cheek comment.

"We brought extra coal and kerosene Shaw. It looks like a long winter is coming up." The old man smiles and nods thankfully.

"And how is Old Reid doing, chap?" utters Lieutenant Blake mockingly to Jim. Shaw stands up and bawls "cut the crap will ye Lieutenant."

"Wow, wow, old man, just kidding my friend. Don't get upset, will you?" Shaw lights his pipe and asks Blake for an update on the Korean War. The news is sobering, and Shaw's face gets serious. Since the end of the Great War when Shaw got out of the army, he still follows what his old Black Watch battalion is involved with. The old man served for nineteen years as a professional soldier. The Lieutenant finishes his second cup of coffee, picks up his cap, and shakes hand with Shaw. The sailors are done unloading and storing the provisions and wait for their commanding officer on the big sloop. Jim companies the officer to the cove.

"I've been hearing voices at night," utters Jim to the Lieutenant. The officer smiles and reassures that the Old Reid story is baloney.

"No, no, Lieutenant, I heard it early this morning again, a kid giggling," mumbles Jim.

"Oh, come on, chap, don't let the nonsense stories get under your skin. It's all folk stories: balahoochie stories as Shaw calls it. Don't worry about it," chuckles the officer.

"Old Banach saw her," continues Jim, "he called her 'bitch' or 'devil' in his logbooks." The officer stops walking and faces Jim.

"Banach left records behind?"

The boy nods, "five volumes written in Polish, but many fragments are in English. I read some of the English fragments." Blake lights another cigarette and thinks for a moment.

"I didn't know Banach. Do you think Shaw will lend them to me? I can have them translated," utters Blake curiously.

"Not a chance Lieutenant, Mr. Shaw keeps them all in his bedroom. The room is like a vault. I got to see the books because I sneaked into his room one day he left to Groats for provisions. He wasn't happy at all I did that." The officer gets rid of the cigarette and continues his way to the cove.

"Shaw told me that the apprentice that drowned was knocked off the cliff by swells. That must have been awful, poor lad," says Jim in a low voice.

The Lieutenant chuckles and replies: "Swells? There were no swells that day! The chap drowned in summer. There are no swells in summer. Sea swells are typically in winter. I don't know why Shaw said that; he should know better!" The officer shakes hand with Jim, goes down the cove, steps in the big sloop, and heads to the Sparrow. A quick ten minutes later the ship pops two short horn blurts and sails away. Jim stands there in deep thoughts.

'If the chap drowned in summer and there are no swells in summer, then why would Shaw say that he was swept away by swells? Somebody isn't telling the truth. Why would Shaw lie to me? Something isn't right.'

The evening fog rolls in and Jim puts the horn in service. As usual his last chore of the day is can duty. His mind is constantly busy deliberating on what Lieutenant Blake told him that morning. The shit-shack is clean, Jim washes his hands, and heads back to the main cottage. He must confront Shaw with what Blake told him about the drowned apprentice.

"Did ye wash yer hands?" mumbles Shaw as usual. Jim doesn't answer the question. He takes off his coat and sits down. Shaw takes the cooking pot off the fire and puts it on the table.

"What's biting ye, lad? Ye look worried. Something bothering ye?" Jim looks at the old man.

"The swells didn't kill the drowned lad," states Jim in a firm voice. Shaw looks at him astonished

"Och, how ye know? Ye're there?"

"He drowned in the summer. There are no swells in summer according to Lieutenant Blake," presses the young man resolutely. Shaw's face turns serious.

"Blake should know when to haud his geggie," mumbles the old man. "Why are you lying to me?" asks Jim sternly. Shaw stirs the pot in silence.

"All that trust and truth preach is nothing but rubbish!" blurts Jim.

"Neay!" hollers Shaw "Ah meant what Ah said."

"And then you lie," rubs Jim in. Shaw puts the pot on the kitchen counter and sits down.

"The lad killed himself. Ah didnae want ye to know that. He jumped off the cliff at night. Ah found his body the following morning in the cove. The lad wasn't gaud in the heid."

"How did you notify the Coast Guard? You had no radio then?"

"That night Ah shot ma flares. Ah have an agreement with the keeper of Duncansby Heid. If he sees flares over Muckle, to immediately call the Guards. He did that and the Guards arrived that night. The deid lad was already bloated. They took him away. Ah told them what Ah think happened; he killed himself. The lad was saying he's going to kill himself if he doesn't leave Muckle. Ah didnae let him gau, and he did what he said. That's why Ah let the second lad leave Muckle. He was saying the same. Ah didnae want to make the same mistake twice." Shaw grabs his pipe and fidgets with it. The boy stands up and walks over to the kitchen counter.

"What made them want to kill themselves?" asks Jim anxiously.

"Ah dinnae ken! They were hearing and seeing things, bogles, and spooks. It's all in their heid!"

"I've heard it! Banach heard and seen it! They have heard it! That can't be coincidence," rebukes Jim immediately.

"Banach was a drunk and the two lads were Jessies! It's the seclusion lad; it works on ye if yer not strong enough. Yer mind starts making things up. It makes its own reality and if yer not strong it will drive ye mad. Banach handled it with Scotch. Ah could bear it 'cause the war hardened me. The two lads couldn't handle the seclusion. Ye can Jim! It's all in yer heid; Ah've seen it before. When ye hear things or see things, just ignore it. Yer mind will stop and settle to reality. It takes grit to dae. Ah know ye can. Ah've seen lads go mad in the trenches. They couldn't block the horror of deid out of their mind. The shelling and deid broke them. It's the same here; the isolation works on ye. Put it out of yer mind and ye'll get used to it. Ah've been here thirty years lad; there are no spooks and bogles. Ah'm sorry Ah didnae tell ye this before. Ah dinnae want to lose ye like the others."

"Banach has been hearing it and seeing it till the end of his days on Muckle. He's been here for thirty years just like you, but he kept hearing it," presses Jim on.

"Banach heard and saw many things when he was drunk. He drank every day! He was a gaud man, but the Scotch made him delirious. He fought devils that were only in his heid."

"I'm not hungry tonight," utters Jim and retires to his room. "It's all in yer heid lad! Ignore it and it will stop!" hollers Shaw. Jim shuts the door.

The night is chilly and the fog quite dense. The south tower beast blurts its low pitch rumble in a steadfast period. Jim can't sleep. The clock shows quarter past eleven. The petrol lamp goes out and Jim lights another one. A rumbling sound of shuffling plates and dishes in the main room catches his attention. *'Is Shaw still awake?'* He grabs the lamp and slowly opens the door. The main room is dark. Jim enters the room: nothing unusual.

"Ye killed yer parents," whispers a female voice. Jim turns around and the hair on his neck stand straight up. "Ye killed yer parents," whispers the voice again. With shaking hands Jim lights another lamp. The room gets better lit: nothing.

"Ye should've gone to the shelter when told," whispers the voice. "Go away" murmurs Jim.

"Neay, Jim, Ah ain't gaun nowhere. Ye know Ah'm right. It's 'cause of ye that yer parents are now deid."

"Go away!" blurts Jim. A creepy giggle fills up the room. Jim lights a third lamp. Shaw opens his bedroom door.

"What the hell is gaun on?" hollers the old man.

"The woman Mr. Shaw, I heard her again. She knows about the death of my parents." Shaw sits down at the table and rubs his face.

"Gau to yer scratcher, lad. Told ye, ignore it; it will stop." Jim stands there wide eyed. The old man stands up and returns to his quarters. Jim grabs all the lit petrol lamps and takes them to his room. The boy sits at the edge of the bed. *'The horn, the horn stopped!'* Jim stands up and puts on his vest, grabs a lamp, and goes into the main room. Shaw is already there putting on his coat.

"The horn lad, it stopped, hurry, let's gau!" The two men step into the courtyard and head to the south tower. A horrifying giggle rips through the night.

"You hear that Mr. Shaw?" asks Jim scared.

"Hear what? Hurry lad, to the horn!" blurts Shaw. The giggle turns into a terrifying laughter.

"Stay here and check the air compressor. Ah'll gau up check the timer," orders the old man. Jim enters the compressor room. The shrieky laughter stops.

"Jim!" utters the female voice. The young man turns around. In the opposite corner he sees a shadow.

"Jim!" says the voice again.

"Go away!" hollers the boy. The shadowy figure steps forward. It's the woman in the portrait: Anne Duncan. Jim's heart races and pounds. The shadowy woman smiles and stretches her arm. In her hand she holds a rose.

"For ye, Jim," she utters in a sweet voice.

"Dinnae forget me, Jim." Suddenly, out of the shadows two little kids step forward. They grab the woman's hand, look at Jim, and smile.

"What the hell are ye waiting for!" hollers Shaw as he bursts into the compressor room. He pushes Jim aside and cranks the compressor engine. The engine starts and soon thereafter the horn resumes its periodic blurting sound.

"What the hell is wrong with ye!" rages the old man. Jim stands there as if hypnotized. Shaw gives him a whack on the back of the head and the boy returns to reality.

"Focus, ma boy!" blurts the old man annoyed.

"The woman in the portrait was here," utters Jim in a quivering voice.

"Rubbish! Get that galoot thing out of yer heid. We're here for the light, remember? In dense fog the horn is even more important than the light! The light gets scattered by the fog, but the sound doesn't. Get a grip lad!" The old man is fuming. Shaw grabs a lamp and rushes out. In a panic the young man follows Shaw back to the cottage. They step into the main room and take off their coats.

"Ye got to stop that havers!" roars the old man.

"When action is needed ye have to take action! Dinnae freeze up. Jings[72] man, get a haud of yerself!" Shaw pours himself a cup of milk.

"Ye want some?" Jim shakes his head and sits down.

"The woman was there, and two kids joined her," babbles the boy incoherently.

"Come on lad, get it out yer heid. Ye're making yerself crazy! There are no bogles here. It's all in yer heid!" hollers Shaw.

"Get some sleep, will ye. That's how the other lads started gaun bonkers on me; they got no sleep." Shaw drinks up the milk, washes the cup, grabs a lamp, and steps into his room.

"Get some sleep!" yells the old man and slams the door shut. The foghorn blurts its belch loudly. Jim stands up, goes to Shaw's door, and knocks softly.

"What?" blurts the old man.

---

[72] Gosh

"May I sleep in your room tonight? I'll sleep on the floor."

The door swings open. "Don't be an eejit, gau to yer scratcher, blow out the lamp, close yer eyes and sleep! The only spooks on Muckle are in yer heid. Now, dinnae be a Jessie and gau!" The door slams shut. Jim grabs all the lamps he can and slowly goes to his room while looking around the room in a paranoid way. The belching foghorn sounds as if it is located next to his ear. The sound keeps bouncing around in his head and the image of Anne Duncan appears as soon as he closes his eyes. There is not much sleep in store tonight.

XVIII

Weeks go by and winter approaches at full speed. Under the close guidance of Shaw, Jim operates all the aspects of the lighthouse lamp. The specter of Anne Duncan and the two kids appear to Jim on several occasions: especially at night in foul weather. Jim works hard at heeding Shaw's advice: just ignore, it's all in his head. However, the ignoring of the apparitions becomes harder and harder. The phantom seems to know all of Jim's past: the death of his parents, the lascivious conduct of the priests and Wobbs at Thebes House, the bamboo canings, and more. She works like a demon, tempting and luring the boy to let her deeper into his soul. The numerous sleepless nights are getting on the young man's nerves. He is edgy and irritated.

One early December day Shaw calls the young man to accompany him to a spot at the most western point of Muckle Skerry. The day is miserably cold, grey, with a light snow falling.

They arrive at a spot where two grey tombstones are placed. On one of the tombstones is engraved:

"In memoriam of nine of the crew of the Vicksburg of Leith, seven of whom are buried here which was wrecked July 17th, 1884"
and on the second tombstone is etched:

"Here lyeth Anne Margarethe Reid, Robert C. Reid, and Peter J. Reid; Wife and two sons of L. Reid P.L.K. 1872 – 1878"

"L. Reid is Auld Reid. Auld folks say he lost his heid after his wife and sons died of a mysterious disease. He just disappeared in thin air," murmurs Shaw. Jim gets the creeps. A woman and two sons, just like the specter and the two young kids, a coincidence?

"Anne Margarethe?" inquires Jim.

"Aye, Anne Margarethe. Auld Burns named his cow Margarethe. Ah have no idea why. Since Burns' Margarethe all cows on Muckle were named Margarethe. Ah dinnae ken why: dark humor, Ah guess." Jim gets this clutching feeling in his stomach.

"Anne and two kids, just what I saw on different occasions appear out of nothing. Coincidence Mr. Shaw?"

The old man taps his forehead and utters, "all in yer heid, lad. Let it gau and it will gau away. Ah thought ye should know about the graves. Next time Blake opens his geggie ye know the graves from me, not him." Shaw fixes his scarf and starts to limp his way back to the lighthouse complex.

"Ah feart the living, lad. Deid people are deid and can't do me a thing. But living ones, that's a different thing." Jim walks silently next to the old man. '*Anne Duncan, Anne Reid, two dead kids, Burns hanged himself, Banach writes about devils and spooks, one apprentice killed himself and the other left scared out of his wits; am I imagining all of this? I didn't know about these graves and still the specter of Anne Duncan and the two kids appear to me. If I'm imagining all this, from where in my mind did the two kids come from, and why?*'

The clutching feeling in his stomach gets worse. The icy wind picks up.

"Storm brooding," utters Shaw and points at the north end of Muckle. The swells are forming. Once in the main room, Shaw shoves more coal into the stove and taps on the barometer hanging on the wall.

"Plunging. Start the horn lad. Ah'll take care of the light; foul weather coming." Jim steps back outside and heads to the foghorn. The snowing gets heavier. The boy enters the compressor room and cranks up the engine. The hammering noise of the engine fills the room. He leaves the compressor room and goes up to the timer-mechanism room upstairs to check on the timer settings. The horn utters its first belch. He enters the room and checks the timer.

"Mommy is mad at ye, Jim," whispers a child's voice. Jim turns around and sees the two kids sitting on a wooden box across the room.

The boys weep and utter again "Mommy doesn't like ye." Jim's heart beats fast but he manages to keep his head straight.

"Tell Mommy to go to hell," replies Jim irritated. The weeping turns into a high pitch giggle.

"Dinnae forget us, Jim," sniggers one of the boys.

"Go away!" hollers Jim loudly. The specters vanish into thin air. The horn hollers and Jim makes a little jump. He hurries back down and returns to the cottage. Shaw is already in the room. He makes a pot of coffee, grabs his pipe, and sits down.

"Skip the can today, lad, weather is too foul," mumbles Shaw.

"I saw the two kids in the timer-room." Shaw doesn't budge.

"They told me their Mommy is mad at me." Shaw stands up.

"Just ignore lad; tell them to piss off!" replies the old man irritated.

"It's gaunnae be nasty tonight. Look at the barometer, haven't seen it this low in many years. It's blizzard low. Put on warm clothes lad, it's gaunnae be freezing."

The wind howls like a choir of wolves. The snow blows practically in horizontal direction. The roof of the cottage cracks and squeaks. Jim desperately tries to catch some sleep. He hasn't got much over the last weeks. The belching horn and the howling wind don't make it easy to sleep. Somehow, in all the infernal noise, Jim slowly falls into a slumber; he is exhausted.

Jim's room at Thebes House is cold. It's snowing outside and Aberdeen is covered white. Herbert, Orville, and Norman are not there. This room at the House is Jim's only. He looks at the clock. It is eleven o'clock at night. Two candles provide a sparse light. Shadows of the desk and chair dance on the walls. There is a soft knock on the door, and it cracks open. It's young Sister Mary. She steps inside and smiles. She silently closes the door behind her.

"Hullo Jim," whispers Sister Mary. Jim, surprised by the unexpected visit, returns the greeting.

"Are you surprised to see me?" asks the Wobb. Jim nods silently.

"I know what happened Jim. You saw me and Father Murray in the library, didn't you?" Jim doesn't respond.

"I'm so sorry Jim, I am here to give you solace. You couldn't help it. He shouldn't have caned you," whispers Sister Mary in a sweet voice. Jim just stands there not knowing what to do.

"I see how you watch me, Jimmy. You're a big lad now. What happened between me and Father Murray is long years ago.

I'm here to explain to you what you saw that night. Now that you're older you should understand and like it. You've been looking at me with a hunger in your eyes. I want to still that hunger tonight: yours and mine." Jim takes a step back.

"Don't be afraid, this is only between you and me." The Wobb takes off her cap and loosens her long thick brown hair. She has a beautiful young face. She approaches Jim and kisses him tenderly on the mouth. Jim's heart beats faster and faster. He senses a bone hard erection growing in his pants. Sister Mary takes a short step back and unbuttons her habit. She drops it on the floor. She's stark naked and smiles. Her body is like that of a goddess.

"I always liked you Jim. You've character. I love strong men." She kneels down and unbuttons Jim's trousers. His body quivers uncontrolled. Suddenly there is a loud bonking on the door. The Wobb stands up and hurriedly picks up her habit and cap. The loud bonking at the door repeats.

"Go in the closet," whispers Jim to the Wobb. She turns around and smiles; it's Anne Duncan.

"Whaaaahhhh!" With a loud scream Jim sits up in bed and his heart races incredibly fast. His underwear is all gooked up with sperm.

"Jim! Dammit! Wake up!" hollers Shaw and bonks hard on the boy's bedroom door. The door is locked.

"Jim! The light went out, hurry!" hollers Shaw while bashing the door even harder. Jim puts on his thick wooly coat and his scarf and opens the door. Shaw is wide eyed.

"Come lad, the light went out!" The wind screeches and howls outside. It's louder than the belch of the south tower beast. They step outside and the snow lashes their face violently. They fight their way against the wind to the north tower. Shaw opens it, steps inside, and quickly shuts the door. The howling wind causes an eerie echoing sound in the tower. The zooming of the mirror engine is muffled by the violent screech of the wind. Shaw hurries up the spiral stairs. Jim stands frozen at the base of the stairs.

"Come on lad! No time to waste!" hollers the old man on his way up. As Jim takes the first steps up he hears a loud thud and a noise of something falling. Suddenly, Shaw appears rolling down the spiral stairs, crashes into Jim, and both roll down to the base of the stairs. Shaw screams in pain. He holds his right leg. A blood stain spreads on his trouser leg. The old man is in agony. Jim frees himself of the weight of the old man and carefully pulls the bloody trouser leg up. Shaw's shin bone protrudes out and the blood gushes out. Jim squints in horror. The old man grabs Jim's arm and in a wild but exhausted voice utters "the light Jim, turn on the light!" The man is in agony. Jim looks at the wound.

"Your leg Mr. Shaw, it's badly broken!" Shaw grabs Jim's arm even firmer.

"Dinnae worry about ma leg. Gau up and no matter what, NO MATTER WHAT, turn on the light! Now!" hollers Shaw full chested. Jim hesitates.

"GAU!" yells the old man in excruciating pain. Jim goes up the spiral staircase. The stairs is icy and slippery. Carefully, Jim makes his way up and reaches the lamp base room. He enters the room and lights two lanterns.

"Ye fancy the young nun, dinnae ye?" whispers a female voice. The boy quickly turns, and the shadowy image of Anne Duncan appears.

"Go away!" hollers Jim.

"Ah know all about the lusty and lewd dreams ye have about Sister Mary," whispers the woman and utters a short giggle. Jim is petrified but he maintains his composure. In a swift move he starts pumping the kerosene mist-generator up.

"I can be yer Sister Mary" giggles the specter.

"Fuck off!" bawls the young man. The woman shrieks a chilling laugh.

"You fancy her gobbling ye just like she did Father Murray, dinnae ye?" hisses the specter and goes into a hysterical laughter. Jim's heart feels like it's going to explode. He tries to block his mind and focus on turning on the lamp. He opens the pilot slot, but the wick is gone. She laughs loudly.

"Are ye looking for this, big boy?" Anne shows him the wick.

"Give me that!" hollers Jim furious. The wench from hell just giggles, opens the window, and throws the wick out.

"NOOOO!" yells Jim. The specter turns and licks her lips and does a blowjob motion. "Go to hell bitch!" blurts Jim.

"Ah am in hell Jimmy, and so are ye!" replies the specter. Jim leaves the base room and goes up to the lamp room to fetch a length of fresh wick. The witch is already up there. The mirror spins around but the lamp is out. She has the wick box. Jim grabs a prodding rod, rushes to the phantom, and swings the rod with full strength. The wick box bursts open and lengths of wick fly all over the place. The woman disappears but a terrifying laughter echoes in the room. Jim cuts a length of wick and hurries back down to the base room. The door to the room is locked. The giggling is incessant.

"Open the door bitch!" The sniggering continues relentlessly. The boy steps back and with his foot tries to ram the door open. The door gives way and Jim stumbles into the room. On the far side of the room he sees the image of Sister Mary standing, completely naked.

"Dinnae ye want me Jim?" whispers the wench. Jim focuses on lighting the wick.

"Jimmy! Jimmy! Ah'm all yers Jimmy! Come and ravage me with yer big hard long wick," mocks the woman and laughs loudly. The wick catches fire! Jim looks at the witch. She blows him a kiss, smiles, and disappears. The boy pumps the mist generator and a few seconds later the light goes on.

"Shaw!" yells Jim and he rushes back down the spiral stairs.

The old man lies unconscious on the floor. His leg is in a pool of blood. In what seems a super human effort, Jim manages to drag Shaw back to the cottage. He lays the old man down on the floor next to the round table. He fetches the scissors and cuts off the trouser leg. The wound is disgusting. He rushes to his room and tunes in the radio.

"Angel[73], Angel, this is Muckle, come in. Angel, Angel, here Muckle, come in!" yells Jim desperately.

"Angel here, come in Muckle," crackles the device.

"Mr. Shaw had an accident. Broke his right leg below the knee. Bone protruding out. Lots of blood." The radio hisses and cracks. "Do you hear me?"

"Got ye Muckle. Is he still bleeding? Over."

"Yes! Over."

"Got to stop the bleeding. Tourniquet the thigh above the knee. Over."

"Tourniquet?"

"Aye! Take a belt and tie the belt around his thigh as tight as possible. That should help stop the bleeding. Over."

"Stand by." Jim unties his belt, ties it around Shaw's thigh and tightens it as much as he can. He rushes back to the radio.

"Angel, Angel, got the tourniquet on. Can you send help? Over."

"Negative Muckle, weather conditions too extreme. Assistance will have to wait for tomorrow."

"What do I do with Shaw?" asks Jim in a rising panic.

---

[73] Code name of Coast Guard base in John o'Groats

"*Monitor the bleeding and keep him warm. Use hot water bottles. If he's in pain use morphine.*"

"Morphine? What's that? Over."

"*Pain killer. Can't do much more than that for now. We'll depart to Muckle as soon as weather conditions permit. Hold fast lad. Angel over and out.*"

Jim drags Shaw to his bedroom, puts him in bed, and makes it as comfortable as possible for the old man. He keeps a watch the whole stormy night.

The following morning the wind calms down, it still snows, and the sea is choppy but no swells. Muckle Skerry is covered in a thick layer of snow, it's icy, and bitter cold. At around nine o'clock in the morning a few sharp horn blows of the H.M.C.G. Sparrow is heard; the Guards are here. Lieutenant Blake and Dr. Dawson, accompanied by a group of sailors, go on shore and hurry through the knee deep snow to the cottage. Jim, weary and exhausted, let them in and ushers Dr. Dawson to Shaw's room.

"It looks bad, lad. Ah'm afraid we have to take him to the hospital in Thurso. He'll have to gau under the knife to fix the shin bone. His heart and breathing are gaud. It's perhaps best for Shaw to be unconscious. When he wakes up the pain will be devilish. Did ye give him morphine?" asks the doctor.

Jim shakes his head in negation "he was out the whole time."

"Let the men bring him to the ship," utters Dr. Dawson to the Lieutenant. The crew brings in a stretcher, put Shaw on it, cover him in thick woolen blankets, and carry him out.

"What happened?" asks Blake.

"The light went out last night. On the way up the spiral stairs he slipped and rolled all the way down. The steps are icy." Lieutenant Blake snuffs out his cigarette.

"Bloody weather. This was a big one; haven't seen something like it in years. There are still more brooding out there. Are you staying here alone, chap?" Jim nods hesitantly.

"You want me to leave two men here? You know in case you need help?" Jim thinks about it for a second and replies "no, Lieutenant, I'll be fine."

It took considerable effort to bring Shaw on board the Sparrow. The iciness, snow, and choppy waters gave the crew a challenge to bring the old man on the ship. However, they managed and now the H.M.C.G. Sparrow heads back to John o' Groats. Jim waves them goodbye. He turns and looks at the lighthouse complex. A chilling feeling gets hold of him. He sighs and heads back to the cottage.

XIX

Days pass by and the she-devil does not appear. Following Banach's account in the logbook, Jim nails self-made wooden crosses to the lighthouse door, the foghorn entrance, the main cottage door, the provision room, and the barn door. *'If it worked for Banach, it should work for me'* reasons Jim. The icy cold and grey clouds hang unwavering over Muckle Skerry. Jim locks his bedroom door at night and places a cross on it. The cross thing seems to work until the night of Christmas Eve 1951.

"Jimmy!" yelps a female voice in the main room. Jim sits straight on the edge of his bed.

"Jimmy! It's Christmas Eve, aren't ye joining us?" It's Anne Duncan, the wench from hell. A cold sweat breaks on Jim's forehead and his heart pulse doubles.

"Come on, laddie, it's the night of joy and peace. Ah'll be gaud tonight" utters the woman and the children giggle. Jim grabs an oil lamp and slowly cracks open the door. The apparitions of the woman and the two boys sit at the round table; they look at Jim and smile. Anne places a red rose on the table.

"My token of peace, luv" utters the woman. The chills run up and down Jim's spine, but he manages to maintain control of his composure.

"What do you want?" inquires Jim.

"We want bigos, luv! Auld Banach used to treat us bigos every Christmas Eve. Aren't ye keeping the tradition?"

"I have no bigos. I don't have dinner. I don't know how to make bigos," utters Jim. The kids emit a loud lament in disappointment. The woman grabs the two kids by the hand, kisses them, and motions them to leave. The youngsters disappear in the shadows. Anne Duncan turns, faces Jim, and smiles.

"Go away," Jim demands. Anne sits down and signals Jim to do the same. Jim's mind is in overdrive. It's all in his head, but it looks so real. The apparition does not look ghostly at all; sitting at the table is a beautiful woman of flesh and blood. The sparkle in her eyes and her mischievous smile are exactly as in the picture. Her dress is old fashioned and so is the jewelry she wears. She taps the table gently and motions Jim to sit down. Jim plays along.

"What is it with all the crosses?" asks Anne Duncan.

"They're supposed to keep you and the kids away from me," answers Jim a bit shaky. Anne snickers and snorts loudly.

"Dinnae be glaikit, lad, all fairy tales and havers. What dae ye take me for?"

"A bitch demon," replies Jim immediately. The specter bursts in laughter.

"Thank ye, Ah'll take that as a complement."

"Did you kill the former apprentice?" asks Jim more resolutely. Somehow his fears of the devilish specter subdue by keep repeating in his mind that it is all an effect of his own imagination.

"Ye mean Charlie?" asks the woman.

"I don't know his name. He drowned," answers Jim.

"Och, aye, Charlie. Wee scunner, a total Jessie," scoffs the specter.

"You killed him?" presses Jim on.

"Neay, luv. He was weak; couldn't handle a real woman. He jumped off the cliff. Ah just showed him the spot, he did the rest," sniggers the wench.

"Go away," rebukes Jim firmly and stands up.

"Not so fast, luv, we have to talk," demands the wench.

"I have nothing to talk to you and don't call me 'luv'; just disappear, I'm not afraid of you."

"Ye remember Elizabeth Tibbs?" asks the woman in a sharp tone of voice.

Jim leans on the table and blurts "go away I said!" The specter leans back and utters a bone chilling giggle.

"Ye dae remember her! She killed herself, ye know?" The boy's face turns cherry red.

"Go away," hollers Jim furious.

"Dae ye want to know why she killed herself?" asks Anne Duncan calmly and smiles.

"No I don't, now piss off!" The specter stands up and comes closer to Jim. He immediately takes a step back.

"Dinnae be feart, luv, Ah dinnae bite," snickers the woman.

"She luved ye, ye know that?" The boy slowly moves away from the specter.

"Father Andrews raped her," utters Jim quietly.

"Neay, Jim. Ye raped her!"

"That's a lie!" hollers the young man furiously.

"She wanted to save her virtue for when she merrit ye, but ye couldn't wait!"

"That's not true! She told me Father Andrews raped her. I never touched the girl except for a kiss!"

"Ye're in denial Jim. Ye ravaged the Tibbs girl summer last year behind the tool shacks. She begged ye to stop, but ye had no ears. Father Andrews never touched Elizabeth; ye did!"

"No! That's not true. I just kissed her. Go away! You're playing my mind!" hollers Jim, goes into his room, and locks the door. The specter softly knocks on the door.

"Jim, luv, it's useless. Ye know it's true. Ye can run, but ye can't hide from me. Ah know everything about ye." A chilling laughter fills the room.

"Piss off!" blurts the young man standing at the closed door.

"Ye're a sneaky bastart, ye know, luv. Ye enjoyed listening to Bishop Carlo fornicate Mother Agnes in the confessional, didnae ye?" giggles the wench.

"Ye knew they were planning to be there that night and ye hid behind the altar. Ye're a sneaky clarty rat. Didnae she moan like a whore?"

"They're all whores, the Wobbs," rebukes Jim.

"Come luv, ravage me like ye did the Tibbs girl; Ah won't kill maself," utters the specter from behind Jim. He turns around and sees Sister Mary under the covers in his bed. She withdraws the covers and she's stark naked. Jim rushes out of the room, enters Shaw's bedroom, opens the trunk, and fetches the handgun. He searches for bullets and finds a box full at the bottom of the trunk. The buy hurriedly loads the revolver and steps back into the main room. The witch sits at the table, fully dressed, rose in hand, and utters a sharp snigger.

"Dinnae be ridiculous, laddie, what ye gaunnae dae with that?" Jim cranks the gun and with a shaky hand shoots at the specter. The recoil of the gun is staunch. The ghost smiles and disappears. Immediately thereafter Jim hears a hellish squealing outside. He fetches the lamp and rushes into the courtyard. The horrid noise comes from the barn. Maggy screeches in a high pitch and so do the pigs and sheep. The chickens cackle loudly.

"Maggy!" yells the boy and he runs to the barn door, slides it open, and steps inside. The squealing stops immediately as Jim slides the door open.

"My God, what have you done?" screams the young man desperately. The animals are chopped to pieces and the barn is smeared in blood. Behind him he hears a wicked cackling. Anne Duncan stands in front of the provision room looking at Jim with beady eyes. Jim blasts a gun shot. The wooden cross on the provision room door splinters to pieces. The cackling turns into a bone chilling laughter.

"Why are you doing this? The poor animals didn't do a thing!" blurts Jim loudly.

"Ah didnae dae a thing Jim. Ye did!" chortles the woman "Look at yer hands." Jim's hands are covered in blood and so are his clothes. The wicked laugh grows louder. Jim kneels. He can't believe what's going on. The loud belching of the foghorn drives him crazy and the evil giggling of the bitch cuts through his head. *'I'm going mad! I'm losing my mind!'* Suddenly the wooden butcher knife case crashes next to him and the knives scatter around. All are drenched in blood. Jim sees the two kids appear in front of the south tower: giggling and snickering. He covers his ears, but the depraved laughter keeps growing louder. The young man stands up and stumbles over to the cottage, goes inside, and slams the door shut.

"Merry Christmas Jimmy," mocks the specter in a loud laughter. Jim drops the gun on the floor. He is exhausted. He sits down and looks at his hands, blood everywhere. The tears fill his eyes and a loud moan bursts out his throat. He stands up and washes his hands and face in the wash bowl. The water turns blood red.

Courtesy of the Muckle Skerry Archives at The John o' Groats Foundation.

"Hi luv," utters the wench. The boy turns and Anne Duncan stands at the main door with the wooden cross in hand. "Let me show ye what Ah dae with this." She lifts her long skirt and brings the cross between her legs, closes her eyes, and utters a soft moan of pleasure. Jim grabs the gun and shoots at her. The specter disappears and the cross drops on the floor. An impish giggle resonates in the room.

"Can't handle the spectacle, Jimmy boy?" echoes the woman's voice. Jim rushes to his room and locks the door. The malicious laughter blares in his head. He puts the gun on the night table, kneels, and passes out on the floor.

The next morning the boy wakes up lying on the floor next to his bed. His head feels as if hit by a rock. It's light outside. The foghorn blurts vigorously. He turns around and his arm tips the night table. The revolver and an empty bottle of allasch fall on the floor. Jim sits up and a sharp sting slices his head. He stands up and wobbles around in the room for a few seconds, opens the door and steps in the main room. The room is a total mess: chairs lay scattered around, the wooden cross is on the floor, and there are bullet holes in the front door and in the kitchen cabinet. The young man stumbles out the main room, heads to the barn, and opens the door. Maggy utters her usual morning 'moo' greeting, the pigs rummage around, and the sheep look at Jim numb eyed. Not a trace of blood. The animals are okay.

"What the hell is going on?" mumbles Jim in unbelieve. The door of the provision room has a bullet hole and the cross is in splinters. Jim staggers back to the main cottage. Another empty bottle of allasch lies in the snow outside. The foghorn belches and the noise bounces around in his head. He rushes to the south tower and turns the horn off, closes the air valves, and sits down utterly exhausted.

"Merry Christmas Jim," murmurs the boy softly. The day is sunny but bitter cold. The young man stumbles back to the cottage, crashes on his bed and passes out exhausted.

XX

Days pass by and the tormenting of the boy by Anne Duncan and kids increase. The young man sleeps poorly and barely eats. The wench from hell is sapping his strengths undeterred by anything or anyone. Jim fights on. The light and the horn must be on. He feels his strength ebbing away but manages to maintain focus on his sole priority, the light. No matter how much he drills his mind that the apparitions are a figment of his imagination, the devil reappears at night in his dreams or around the complex. Doors rattle, windows burst open, pans and pots in the kitchen tumble down from the racks, Shaw's bookcase was toppled, and the kids from hell are on a rampage. One evening in mid-January 1952, the radio crackles and a call comes in from the Coast Guard in John o' Groats.

"*Muckle, Muckle, come in, Angel here, [silence, crackling sounds], Muckle, Muckle, come in, Angel calling.*"

Jim steps in his room and replies, "Angel, Muckle here, over."

"*Muckle, Shaw is being discharged from hospital. We will bring him to Muckle tomorrow morning. Weather forecast looks good. Over.*"

A big smile appears on Jim's face; the old man is coming back!

"Angel, that is great news! The old man is strong. Is he walking already? Over."

"*I have Dr. Dawson here. He wants to talk to ye, stand by.*" More crackling sounds on the radio.

"*Jim? Ye there?*"

"Yes, doctor, I'm here, over."

"Jim, the shin is healing good, but Ah've some bad news." Somehow, the boy feels that what's coming is serious and braces for it.

"What's the matter, doctor, over."

"Tests made during Shaw's stay in the hospital at Thurso are positive; Shaw has lung cancer. He is beyond any medical treatment. We give him not more than six months. Ah'm sorry lad but thought ye should know in advance." Jim's heart shrinks to the size of a pea. The old man is dying. He can't believe it.

"Thank you for informing me, doctor, over and out." *'Click'*. Jim switches off the radio. He lays down his bed and stares at the roof beam straight above his head. The bad news slowly sinks in and a rush of sad emotions emerges in Jim's soul. This is completely unexpected. The old man is dying, just unbelievable. Before the accident he was strong like a horse! Tears well up in his eyes. The old man is stern, a disciplinarian, heavy handed sometimes, stubborn like an ass, but he was never unfair and always well giving. *'I've learned a lot from him in one short year.'* Jim hears the clock ticking and looks at it; it is fifteen minutes to four. The winter sun is setting, and he must turn on the light. The weather is clear but still bitter cold. There is no need for the horn tonight and Jim is thankful for that. He puts on his winter coat, leaves the cottage, and heads to the light tower. Inside the tower is dark. He lights a lamp and starts his way up the spiral stairs. About halfway up he notices a shadow sitting on the stairs half a dozen or so steps above him. Fear engulfs his heart. It's the witch Anne Duncan and her two brats from hell.

"Don't waste yer time, luv, the light ain't gaun on tonight," utters the specter. Jim's heart pounds like a sledgehammer in his chest. *'It's all in my head. Focus Jim, the light.'* Jim continues his way up as if there is nothing impeding his way. The wench slowly stands up and does not budge.

"Where ye gaun, laddie?" inquires the devil woman. Jim continues his way up. In a lightning quick move the woman grabs the boy by the throat and presses him against the wall. Her strength is superhuman.

"There's no light tonight, boy!" hollers the ghost in a deep horrid groan. Jim grabs the woman's choking hand in an attempt to free himself. The hand is ice cold. She brings her face close to Jim's. Her eyes are blood red and her breath reeks of rotten flesh. The kids start crying "dinnae hurt him Mommy, dinnae hurt him."

"He's coming back, isn't he Jimmy?" The strangling iron grip of the demon presses the air out of the boy. He can't utter a single word. The wench pushes Jim down and he rolls down a few steps of the stairs. The boy stands back up, catches his breath, and notices a streak of blood running down his face. He has a cut on his forehead. The witch laughs loudly and the little monsters giggle.

"Yer teacher is coming back tomorrow, isn't he luv?" growls the woman in a devilish voice.

"Yes bitch! Nothing is stopping me putting the light on, so get out of my way!" roars Jim. The witch utters a loud shriek and cackles an evil laugh.

"Ye've got guts, laddie, Ah like that, men with character! But there will be no light tonight 'cause Ah said so!"

"Fuck you!" bawls Jim and rushes up the stairs. The bitch grabs him by his jacket collar and hurls him back down. Jim tumbles down hard but manages to grab the handrail.

"Leave Muckle Skerry lad, ye've nothing to seek here! Ye either leave walking like the former lad or deid like Charlie! But ye'll leave!" threatens the woman. Jim stands up. It's a wonder the oil lamp in his hand is still intact. *'This can't be just my imagination? The bitch bashes me at will!'* Jim puts the lamp down on the step, kneels, and starts to pray. The fear is deep, but he stands his ground.

"The Lord is my Light and salvation — whom shall I fear? The Lord is the stronghold of my life — of whom shall I be afraid? One thing I ask from the Lord, this only I seek: that I may dwell in the house of the Lord all the days of my life, to gaze on the beauty of the Lord and to seek him in his temple. He maketh me lie down in green pastures: he leadeth me beside the still waters. He restoreth ma soul: he leadeth me in the paths of righteousness for his name sake. Surely goodness and mercy shall follow me all the days of my life: and Ah will dwell in the house of the Lord forever. The Lord is my strength and guardian in the battles that lyeth before me. He shall not leave me alone in the face of evil. Whoever dwells in the shelter of the Most High will rest in the shadow of the Almighty. I will say of the LORD, He is my refuge and my fortress, my God, in whom I trust. Amen."

In a loud roar Jim lurches up the stairs and with almost superhuman strength he shoves the bitch from hell aside and grabs one of the brats in a headlock. Anne Duncan's eyes grow big and her face changes into a greyish color. Her beautiful face turns into that of a monstrous demon. The kid tries to free himself but at no avail. The she-devil grabs Jim by the hair and yanks him to her, but the young man manages to fix a punch square on her nose. She stumbles back wide eyed and astounded by the boy's strength. Jim throws the kid down the stairs.

"No!" hollers the witch and attacks Jim in full force. The young man grabs a hold of her and both stumble down the spiral stairs. The boy hits his head hard on the floor and loses consciousness.

Jim regains consciousness with a splitting headache. He staggers up. The tower is dark and there is no trace of the she-devil and her brats. "The light! I must turn on the light," murmurs Jim quietly. Carefully he feels his way up the stairs in the dark. About halfway up he finds the oil lamp and lights it. As the stairway is filled with light, he notices an empty bottle of allasch placed a few steps up. *'What the hell? I didn't touch the stuff!'* He touches his forehead and indeed there is a bleeding cut on it. He shakes his head and continues his way up the stairs. Jim enters the base room and lights two more lanterns. He checks the pilot wick. It's there and it's ready for service. Slowly the boy pumps up the kerosene mist generator. At the right pressure he opens the small butterfly valve and lights the wick. The system utters a hissing sound and a red glow appears upstairs in the lamp room. He goes upstairs to the lamp room and starts the engine that drives the rotating mirror. In a bright flash the three lamps turn intense white. The light is on! Jim smiles, but his body is in pain from the fall. He checks the gearbox, leaves the light room, and makes his way down to ground level. It's dark and quiet in the courtyard. *'What on earth happened?'* asks Jim. He remembers fighting feverishly against the witch. His head feels hung over and his body aches everywhere. Did he drink the allasch? Was the fight a drunk's delirium? He can't remember a thing of drinking allasch. His mind is blank except for the fight in the tower. Jim enters the main cottage and lights the oil lamps. An empty bottle of allasch lies on the table. *'What the hell is going on? I can't recall having a single drink of allasch!'* He opens the stove and shoves one more wooden cross in it. He removed all the crosses. The crosses didn't have any effect in keeping the witch away.

"Jimmy! Where are you. Don't hide. Come we have to hurry to the bomb shelter!" The boy freezes up. It's her mother's voice in the same panicky tone as on that dreadful night in London.

"Jimmy! Come out now!" It's his father's thundering voice. Suddenly, sirens holler loudly and fill the room with that terrible feeling of the night during the Blitz in 1940. The boy covers his ears and screams, "Stop! I know it's you bitch!" The blaring wail gets louder.

"Jimmy, Jimmy, hurry we must go!" Jim squats down in agony.

"Jim, where are you! Come out now, we have to go to the shelter!" hollers his father's voice. Abruptly, the floor starts to shake and the thundering sound of bombs exploding is heard. "Jimmy! Hurry, come out, please!" begs his mother. Jim lies down on the floor.

"STOP!" hollers the boy desperately. Suddenly, the noise stops, and all is quiet. A wicked snigger fills the main room.

"Ye killed yer parents, Jimmy," utters the witch.

"It was all yer fault. If ye didnae hide like a Jessie yer parents would be alive and ye wouldn't be here in hell with me," chuckles the wench. Jim opens his eyes and sees the witch sitting at the table. She stretches her arm offering the boy a red rose.

"I was scared. I was six years old for god's sake!" yells the young man.

"Ye were, and are, a Jessie!" rebukes the witch. Jim stands up, wipes the tears, and sits at the table opposite of her.

"What do you want of me?"

"Ah want ye to leave Muckle and never come back," answers the specter. "Gau to India or Australia like ye always wanted. But leave Muckle forever!"

"Why? I've no quarrel with you?"

"Anybody who helps Shaw has a quarrel with me!" blurts the woman angrily.

"What's your problem with the old man?"

"He murdered ma boys and me," says the ghost in a hateful tone of voice. Jim looks her straight in the eyes. Tears pour down her cheeks. The witch's face is utterly sad and full of hate.

"He's ma husband. Ah'll make him pay for all he has done!" utters the creature from hell.

"That can't be, Shaw never married," replies Jim firmly.

"Is that what the clarty liar told ye? And ye believed him? Ye're more of a gowk than Ah thought," sniggers the wench.

"Anne Duncan married a man from Glasgow during the Great War. He showed me the letter she wrote him in 1917," rebukes Jim. The witch looks intensely at the boy and slowly breaks a smile.

"And who told ye Ah'm Anne Duncan?" inquires the wench.

"He did. You're the woman in the portrait!" The witch stands up and utters a wicked laugh.

"Ye're worse than eejit Charlie. At least he had the guts to jump off the cliff. Get off this island, laddie, or ye'll suffer the same fate as eejit Charlie!" hisses the woman. Jim doesn't flinch.

"Look outside, luv, where is yer so beloved light?" The boy stands up and hurries to the kitchen window. The light is off.

"You turned off the light, you bitch!" The woman shrieks an evil laugh and disappears. Jim grabs his coat and hurries out in the courtyard. Indeed, the light is out.

"Bitch!" hollers Jim furiously. The two brats from hell appear out of nothing and run to the lighthouse door. They turn into huge dogs with fiery red eyes and stand guard at the lighthouse door, snarling, growling, and showing their teeth. Jim hurries back in the cottage and fetches Shaw's handgun. He steps outside and shoots at the canine monsters. Nothing happens, the two Cerberus stand their ground. The wench laughs and shrieks. The boy drops the gun and climbs up the gutter pipe to the cottage roof. If he gets to the tower window, he can make it in the light tower. The two hell dogs bark, growl, and scratch the cottage wall.

Jim hops from roof to roof towards the window. The bitch and the kids suddenly appear standing in front of the tower window.

"Where ye think yer gaun, eejit?" sniggers the witch. Jim freezes. He kneels down and prays. Without any hesitation the witch whacks Jim a kick in the face, he rolls down the roof, and smacks on the ground.

"Eejit!" yelps the wench. The hellish dogs reappear on the ground and attack Jim. He tries to defend himself with all his might, but the two Cerberus are fierce and unbending.

"Oh God! Help me!" hollers the poor young man. The witch laughs incessantly. Suddenly, out of nowhere, there is a loud thunder. A bold of lightning hits the tower, and the light miraculously turns on. The hell-dogs stop mauling Jim, and the wench looks up. The two Cerberus utter a monstrous howl and the witch emits a terrifying scream. They turn into dust and disappear into the nothing. Jim drags himself into the cottage. The demon dogs mangled him quite bad. His arms and legs are bitten and bloody. He grabs the medicine box and pours sulfur on the wounds. It burns horribly. The boy manages to sit down at the table and bandages his arms and legs. Jim looks at the clock; it is half past two in the morning. He passes out.

XXI

A week goes by. Shaw is back on Muckle Skerry. He moves around in a wheelchair and he hates it. Shaw behaves strange and is very quiet. The leg is still bandaged. Dr. Dawson explicitly told him that he must not put load on the leg. The only thing Shaw does is cook. He feels himself useful doing that. Jim takes care of everything else. Supper is ready and Jim is back from doing the can.

"Did ye wash yer hands?" asks Shaw resolutely.

"Yes, Mr. Shaw." Jim utters the usual answer. The old man wheels around the kitchen and is visibly irritated that he's condemned to the chair. He scoops the meal and does the prayers.

"Ye look like keech, lad. Ye lost weight and are all mangled up. What happened?" asks Shaw calmly. Jim doesn't answer.

"Ye've been on the bottle, haven't ye?" asks Shaw. Jim doesn't budge.

"Ah had twenty-five bottles of allasch. Two we drank up. Now there are only fourteen. Did ye drink them?" Jim puts down the spoon.

"I can't remember touching the stuff," rebukes Jim.

"Did the bottles just walk away?" snaps the old man. Jim remains quiet.

"Ye disappoint me lad," utters the old man in a low voice.

"I didn't touch the allasch!" bawls Jim angrily.

"Where did the bottles gau? Ye sold them in Groats?" asks Shaw sarcastically.

"I don't know," answers Jim.

"Ye've been messing around with ma gun too," states Shaw in a quiet tone.

"Yes, Mr. Shaw. I won't lie to you." The old man puts down his spoon and looks at Jim with piercing eyes.

"What happened?"

"The devil was here," answers the boy softly. Shaw wheels back his chair and grabs the pipe.

"Tell me," utters the old man. Jim remains quiet.

"Ye saw her again?" murmurs Shaw. Jim nods.

"What happened?" asks the old man again.

"She told me she is your wife," utters Jim. Shaw wheels the chair further back and lights the pipe.

"Gau on," he utters.

"She snuffed the light. I fought her and the hell boys." Shaw remains quiet.

"It's not my imagination! She's real!" utters Jim anxiously.

"She told me you murdered her and the two boys." Shaw, in a rage, throws the pipe at Jim.

"What kind of galoot story is that?! Ah told ye Ah never merrit!" Jim stands up and puts his plate in the wash bowl.

"That's what she told me," affirms the boy.

"Yer fancy is out of control lad!" bawls Shaw. The boy washes his hands and disappears into his room. A few seconds later the rickety-click of the battery charger is heard. Shaw wheels around the table, picks up his pipe, blows out the lamps, and goes to bed.

Days, and weeks pass by and the old man is visibly deteriorating. The wench from hell did not reappear. Even the cooking became a gargantuan task for Shaw. He forgot things, misplaced things, and becomes disoriented quickly. Jim tries his best to make the best for the old man. One night, after dinner, Jim couldn't hold in anymore.

"You have lung cancer. Did they tell you?" asks Jim in a low voice. Shaw remains quiet. "Well?" presses Jim.

"Yes, they did. Dr. Dawson told me. Ah can't dae a thing. Ah'm rotting away," utters Shaw. His voice quivers. His face is sad. He's not the Shaw of a year ago.

"I will take good care of you, Mr. Shaw, I promise." Shaw looks at the young man and his eyes get all misty.

"Ah nair[74] expected to gau this way."

---

[74] never

Jim looks at him and replies, "we all have to go some way." A crooked smile appears on Shaw's face.

"Ah hope that when Ah face the Lord Ah can stand on ma own." The old man taps the wheelchair.

Jim smiles, "you will," answers the young man. Shaw utters a snigger and Jim laughs.

"Bring out the chess set! Ah want to skelp yer bahookie before Ah die!" hollers the old man. Jim goes into his room and fetches the chess set.

"Ye play white," utters Shaw. The game begins. Midway the game Shaw topples his king for no reason.

"What are you doing?" shrieks Jim. Shaw remains quiet. He picks up the black queen and looks intensely at it. The old man's eyes fill with tears and his stare at the black queen turns icy. Without uttering a word, Shaw puts the queen on the table and slowly puts two black pawns next to her: one pawn on each side of the queen.

"Are you alright?" asks the boy softly. The old man does not budge and with teary eyes he keeps gazing at the three chess pieces. Tears roll down the man's cheeks. Jim has never seen Shaw this way. The agony, the pain, the grief he experiences is clearly visible on his face.

"Fate is harsh and graceful. The Lord is ma Light and strength; who shall Ah be afraid of?" Shaw wheels back his chair, smiles, goes into his room, and slowly closes the door. Jim looks puzzled at the black queen with the two pawns on the table. The old man wanted to tell the boy something: something like a confession. The three chess pieces give Jim an eerie feeling. He gathers the pieces and puts them in the box.

XXII

The entrance hall of Thebes House is damp and murky. As usual the hall is dimly lit by the dozens of candles on the big oak table in front of the large crucifix. The summer weather in Aberdeen is clammy due to an unusual high humidity. Jesus hangs on the cross, emaciated, bloody, and with the customary stare in his glassy eyes. Jim does the cross sign and sits on the bench across the hall. It is midday and the sun is shining, but the entrance hall is somber and gloomy.

"Why am I here?" whispers Jim. Jesus doesn't answer.

"Jim?" calls a high-pitched voice. Jim stands up and focuses his eyes on two shadowy figures standing in the hallway to the stairs.

"Jim, is that you?" utters the voice again. Norman and Orville appear out of the shadowy hallway. Jim smiles and rushes over to his former roommates and give them a hug.

"Norman, Orville, I've missed you guys. Where is Herbert?" asks Jim surprised. The two lads look at each other and Norman replies, "he was discharged a month ago."

"Where did he go?" inquires Jim.

"We don't know. He wouldn't tell us. He wasn't happy about it though. He said it's a place that is far away," answers Norman.

"Did Father Murray go with him? Maybe I can ask him?" Norman and Orville look at each other again and shake their head.

"No. The police picked Herbert up early in the morning. We saw him from the window step into the police car and drive away. There were no Wobbs and no priests present."

"The police?" asks Jim anxiously. The two boys nod.

"Did he do something wrong?"

"Not that we know of," replies Orville. Jim sits down on the bench. He can't believe what he is hearing.

"It is nice seeing you again Jim. We have to go now. The Wobbs are really nervous the last few weeks. Something happened, but we don't know what. The police took Mother Agnes too, but after a couple of hours she came back." The friends hug and say goodbye. Norman and Orville hurry up the stairs. Jim slowly approaches hanging Jesus.

"What happened to my friend?" asks Jim in a low voice.

"He raped Elizabeth Tibbs," answers a male voice. Jim takes two steps back and his heart rate ramps up out of control. Jesus turns his head and looks straight at the boy.

"Herbert did a very bad thing and now he's paying for it. You should pay too! He tried to do the same thing you did to the Tibbs girl" grunts the hanging son of God. A cold sweat breaks all over Jim. What the hell is going on?

"That's impossible! Elizabeth is dead," utters Jim in a low and shaky voice. Jesus yanks his hands and feet from the nails and climbs down from the cross. The divine man wipes the blood from his hands with the table cloth, brushes off the candles from the oak table, grabs the table cloth, and puts it over his half naked body.

"The Tibbs girl didn't die after you did what you did to her," utters Jesus while walking around the table. Jim hurries back to the bench.

"I did not do a thing wrong to Elizabeth! I just kissed her," asserts Jim firmly. Jesus walks over to the front door, grabs the door handle, and cracks the door open. The sunlight and the street buzz enter the hall. The son of God looks at Jim.

"Many months ago you sat there and asked me why I don't just climb down the cross and leave. Well, that day has come. This place is rotten, putrid, and evil. So are you Jim. You should join the

Reid woman in hell, just like her husband did." Jesus steps out the door and with a forceful yank shuts the big front door. The thunderous bang of the shutting door reverberates through the large hall.

Jim sits straight up in bed, sweaty and panting. *'What a weird dream was that'* he ponders. A rolling thunder resounds, and the window panes vibrate. It is June and the summer thunder storms are starting to make their presence felt. Jim looks at the clock. It's eleven o'clock at night. The wind blows strong and the rain clatters on the window. The cottage roof squeaks and cracks. He sits on the edge of the bed and looks at himself in the mirror. The shadowy figure he sees in the mirror is barely visible. A lightning flash appears followed immediately by a loud thunder clap. The lighthouse is probably getting a beating again. Jim's mind wanders over to the old man's health condition. His condition is worsening. His breathing is laborious, and he coughs up blood. The stubborn Scot refuses any treatment to relief the pains. He has been in bed for the last three weeks, barely eating and very silent. Jim does his best to take good care of the old man. However, the rapid decline in Shaw's health saddens the young man almost to the point of succumbing to a mental depression. The old man is stern, a disciplinarian, stubborn like an ass, but he has grown to be a father figure to Jim; something he never had since the death of his parents. Jim knows the old man is dying, but he hopes to make his last days as best as he can. Shaw had nights of unbearable pain and the boy had to suppress the pain with morphine. Some days, when Shaw feels better, he wheels around the main room as if looking for something useful to do. However, his roaming around is of no avail. The cruel illness saps his strength and makes every attempt to make himself useful futile. Especially that, his realization that he cannot do the things he loves to do, infuriates and saddens the old man at the same time.

Jim lights a petrol lamp and goes into the main room. The slit underneath Shaw's bedroom door is lit. *'Is the old man awake?'* asks Jim to himself. He hears a mumbling sound coming from Shaw's room. The young man slowly walks over to the door and eavesdrops. The mumbling is a soft sobbing.

"You killed father, Mommy," utters a sad child's voice. The sobbing continues. Jim's eyes grow wide and his heart rate accelerates up fast. It's the voice of one of the kids from hell.

Courtesy of The Anne Duncan Institute, Aberdeen.

Besides the sobbing, a soft sniggering is heard; it's the creepy snorting of Anne Duncan.

"Mr. Shaw!" hollers Jim. The room immediately goes quiet. Jim grabs the door handle and tries to open the door, but it's locked. Shaw never locks the door since he returned from the hospital.

"Mr. Shaw!" hollers Jim again while trying to force the door open. A wicked laugh creeps its way from inside the locked bedroom into the main room. Jim bangs, pulls, and pushes the door but it won't budge. The moaning and sobbing of the kids grows louder. The boy hurries to his room and fetches the pincer and the bend nail to pick the door lock. The moaning, sobbing, and the wicked giggling fill up the room. The young man kneels at the door and with trembling hands tries to pick the lock. The sobbing and giggling turn into a monstrous groan. The thunderstorm grows fiercer and a barrage of lightning strikes hit the lighthouse complex. The groan turns into a loud growl like that of a furious beast.

"Hold on Mr. Shaw! I'm here. I'll help you!" yells Jim in a frantic tone of voice. Finally, the lock yields and Jim bursts into Shaw's bedroom. Suddenly, the growling stops, and the lightning barrage eases away. Jim can't believe his eyes.

"No, no, no, not like this," utters Jim softly and kneels down. He bursts into an uncontrollable weeping and puts his hands in front of his face. Sitting at the head of the bed is Shaw; his eyes and mouth are wide open. He is dressed in his Black Watch uniform. The wall and Banach's painting hanging on top of the bed head is splattered with blood. The Enfield revolver lays on the old man's lap, his hand still holding the gun. The old man shot himself through the mouth. Except for the sound of the rain and wind, the dimly lit room is quiet. It seems that even the thunder and lightning ceased. Jim still cannot believe it. That awkward feeling of utter loneliness overwhelms him again. He heard the witch and the kids, but now there is not a single trace of them. With great difficulty Jim gets his emotions under control. He wipes the tears from his face, stands up, walks slowly over to the body of the old man, and gently closes his eyes. The boy removes the revolver from Shaw's hand and places it on the floor. On the night table stands the woman's portrait and next to it lies a sealed envelope. On top of the envelope are placed three chess pieces: the black queen, and two black pawns. Next to the envelope lies a red rose. The envelope is addressed to Jim.

Jim, ma gaud frein,

When ye read this letter, Ah've joined ma long-gone lads in a world beyond this one. Ah can only hope ye forgive me. Ah could not bear it anymore. Ah've done much bad in ma life and ma time of reckoning has come. The wars Ah fought were aglea. They haunt me every day and every night. But the wars themselves were not ma punishment; surviving them is. Ah nair thought Ah would end this way, but this way is best. All Ah ask from ye is this: 1) please bury me next to Anne Reid's grave, 2) bury me in full uniform with ma guns, medals, and bagpipe, 3) no crosses, no headstone, no priest. Please, do yer frein a last favor.

Jim, Ah nair had a family of ma own, but ye are the closest Ah ever got to having a son. Keep the Light, ma son, and ye'll be set free. The redemption for my sins Ah have to seek in the Lord's temple. He is ma Light and strength; whom shall Ah feart? Remember me when ye wash yer hands. We shall meet again in green pastures with clear waters. Please, forgive me and thank ye ma dear frein.

Lewis Shaw.

Tears fill up Jim's eyes. He folds the letter and puts it back in the envelope. Jim accommodates Shaw's remains on the bed and covers the body with a large blanket. He fetches the black queen and the two pawns and look intensely at them. The strange and eerie feeling returns. Jim looks at the rose. "Where did Shaw get the red rose?" whispers Jim and looks at Anne Duncan's portrait. The mischievous smile of the woman seems more pronounced than before. An air of gloating and fulfillment radiates from the portraited woman. Jim blows out the lamps and heads to his room.

"Angel, Angel, come in, Muckle here," utters Jim in the microphone.

"Angel here, over," crackles a voice on the radio.

"Lewis Shaw is dead."

XXIII

The H.M.C.G. Sparrow is anchored at Muckle Skerry on the 16th of June and all is prepared for Shaw's last farewell. The old man is dressed in his Black Watch uniform, medals pinned, rifle and gun placed, and his bagpipe put carefully underneath his folded hands. Jim is meticulous at that. The casket is closed, and the crew carries it from the lighthouse complex to the western edge of Muckle Skerry: the grave site. It's a grey cloudy June day and the seagulls are loud and plentiful. Lieutenant Blake, Dr. Dawson, and the Sparrow crew attend; there is no priest. The fresh dug grave next to the Reid woman is ready. The casket is put on top of the grave on two wooden beams and the lowering ropes are passed underneath. Jim fetches a piece of paper and reads:

"The Lord is my Light and salvation — whom shall I fear? The Lord is the stronghold of my life — of whom shall I be afraid? One thing I ask from the Lord, this only I seek: that I may dwell in the house of the Lord all the days of my life, to gaze on the beauty of the Lord and to seek him in his temple. May Mr. Shaw's soul rest in peace in the temple of the Lord. Amen."

Some of the crewmen do the sign of the cross. Jim nods his head and the wooden beams are removed. The wind blows starkly, and the gulls are noisy. Lieutenant Blake nods to a sailor and he steps forward. He puts a bagpipe under his arm and plays, in long melancholic notes, the song *We were Soldiers*[75] while the other lads slowly lower the casket down into the cold-cold ground. The Lieutenant and the rest of the crew salute. The song ends, the casket lies in the grave, and the ropes are thrown over the casket.

"Remove the crucifix," orders Jim. Blake looks at him wide eyed.

"The crucifix on the casket, remove it!" commands the young man. Blake motions a sailor to jump in the grave and remove the cross. The sailor does so. A light drizzle starts to fall. The skies are dark grey. Jim grabs a handful of sand and tosses it on the casket. Blake, Dr. Dawson, and the crew follow. The boy nods and the crew starts filling up the grave.

"I will contact the war office to make a headstone for the man," offers Blake.

"No! No headstone. He wanted it this way," asserts Jim immediately. Blake acknowledges. The grave is filled up and the crew and Dr. Dawson head back to the ship. Blake and Jim remain at the grave.

"Are you staying on Muckle?" asks Blake in a low voice. Jim answers "yes."

---

[75] Scottish song in tribute to fallen comrades

"Are you sure about that chap?" repeats Lieutenant Blake. The boy looks at him, smiles, and nods. Blake stretches his hand and says:

"Godspeed chap. You can always count on us." The young man shakes his hand and the Lieutenant heads back to the Sparrow. The boy stands there for a few minutes listening to the wind and the seagulls. He turns and heads back to the lighthouse complex.

At the cottage Jim makes Shaw's bed square and meticulous; like Shaw himself would have done. He sits on the edge of the bed, picks up the portrait of the woman holding a rose, takes off the frame, and takes a good look at the woman in the photograph. The woman's face is beautiful, but it is not that of the witch. The woman pictured is somebody else. On the back side of the photograph is a handwritten note that says:

Godspeed my love. Always loving you. Anne Duncan. Inverness, May 12, 1916.

Jim steps into the main room photograph in hand. He opens the black stove, shoves the woman's photograph in the fire, and whispers "may you now rest in peace, Anne Margarethe Reid."

※ ※ ※ ※

James Evans P.L.K. was the last Principal Lighthouse Keeper of Muckle Skerry. He tended the light for 42 years, the longest lighthouse keeper ever on the island. In 1994, the lighthouse on Muckle Skerry was fully automated and there was no need any more for a full-time lighthouse keeper. That year Jim departed from Muckle Skerry and never returned.

Orville Watson, one of the former roommates of James Evans at the Thebes House, and now a retired BBC journalist, made it his quest to find out what happened to his former fellow orphan roommates. Herbert Huckelbee just disappeared from the face of the earth. Orville couldn't find a trace of him. Norman Bale settled down in Glasgow, became a businessman, and made a fortune. From the records of the Northern Lighthouse Commission Orville could trace that Jim left Muckle Skerry in 1994. After years of researching ship and flight records, Watson traced Jim back to a small town in northern Sri Lanka. Watson travels to Sri Lanka and guided by a local man he ends up at a small graveyard located at the northern tip of the island. Orville's guide is called Prakaash. He escorts the former journalist to a small and barely noticeable tombstone on which is engraved: *"Sassenajee, Protector of Light".*

"Here he rests," utters Prakaash in his heavy Indian accent.

"What was he like?" Orville asks the man.

"He was a very wise man. He never told us his real name. He only told us that he's from England and to call him *Sassenajee*. If he wasn't English, he would have been a revered guru. He came out of nowhere. Settled down in town and built a school for the young with his money. Sassenajee always said, there is no greater power than love, and the source of love is the Light, the light of wisdom, the light of knowledge, the light of tolerance, the light of friendship, and the light of compassion. Love each other, help each other, and trust each other, no matter Jew, Christian, Buddhist, Muslim, Hindi, or whatever gender, creed, politics, or race. We're all here for a brief moment; make it matter in a positive light. Where we live is where the Light shines. We miss him very much." The man goes silent and Orville can sense his sadness.

"Did he have scars on his back?" asks the retired journalist.

"Yes, many gruesome scars on his back, arms, and legs. He said he got them fighting the devil." Orville notes it down in his notebook.

"What else can you tell me about Sassenajee?" The man stares at the grave.

"The only thing he asked for is that we honor his memory every 11th hour on November the 11th, bring him a red rose, and put it on his grave. That's all. He was a great man." Orville notes that in his book; the date is June 15th, 2023.

"Supper is ready. Do you care to join us?" asks Prakaash.

"Of course! Love the local food," answers Orville cheerfully.

"Did you wash your hands?" asks the guide. Orville looks at him surprised and answers, "no, but I will."

"Good! Let's eat!" answers Prakaash cheerfully. Jim, the Sassenach Principal Lighthouse Keeper of Muckle Skerry, fulfilled his dream. Let there be Light for evermore.

THE END.

Milton Keynes UK
Ingram Content Group UK Ltd.
UKHW011818111223
434184UK00003B/279